Almost Home

Almost Home

A novel by

Nora Raleigh Baskin

LITTLE, BROWN AND COMPANY

New York ⌐ An AOL Time Warner Company

ALSO BY NORA RALEIGH BASKIN:

What Every Girl (except me) Knows

Copyright © 2003 by Nora Raleigh Baskin
Reader's Guide copyright © 2005 by Nora Raleigh Baskin
and Little, Brown and Company (Inc.)

Little, Brown and Company

Time Warner Book Group
1271 Avenue of the Americas, New York, NY 10020
Visit our Web site at www.lb-teens.com

First Paperback Edition: September 2005

Library of Congress Cataloging-in-Publication Data

Baskin, Nora Raleigh.
Almost home : a novel / by Nora Raleigh Baskin. — 1st ed.
p.   cm.
Summary: After years of being shuffled from town to town and back and forth between
her divorced parents, twelve-year-old Leah, now living permanently with her father and
stepmother, finds it difficult to adjust to her new situation and the circumstances that
made it possible.
ISBN 0-316-09313-0 (HC) / ISBN 0-316-01028-6 (PB)
[1. Family problems — Fiction.   2. Stepmothers — Fiction.   3. Friendship — Fiction.
4. Self-acceptance — Fiction.]   I. Title
PZ7.B29233 Al 2003
[Fic] — dc21   2002028297

10 9 8 7 6 5 4 3 2 1

Q-FF

Printed in the United States of America

The text was set in Perpetua and Clyde, and the display type is Rodin

With much love and thanks to

My editor, Maria Modugno, once again.

Elinor Lipman and Mameve Medwed, not just for
understanding but for coming through.

Mr. John Thomsen, my *real* sixth-grade language
arts teacher, who made a *real* difference in my life.

My young, first readers and supporters (a growing list),
Erin *and* Brigit Anderson, Kristin *and* Kelsey Millay, Daniel
and Greg Berger, Arielle Cutler, Erica Berlin, Alexander
Pachman (for the name help), and Ben Simpson
(who pointed out that school buses
do not have green vinyl seats anymore).
And to any and all of my students who
would consent to listen.

My family (all configurations), for the memories
and for the stories.

And to Steve, Sam, and Ben, with all my heart.

— N.R.B.

"You can't always get what you want.
But if you try sometime, you just might find—
You get what you need."

—JAGGER/RICHARDS, THE ROLLING STONES

For my sister, Anne

Almost Home

Chapter One

The bus ride was making me sick. Mrs. Thomsen said it was only a half an hour to the Roosevelt Mansion, but I think we'd been on the bus for an hour already. Everybody had their windows open, but mine was stuck and I didn't want to ask anyone for help.

I didn't know anybody.

So I just looked out the window. I was thinking of everything that, if I could, I would tell my mother. I would tell her about this field trip, and my new teacher, and everything I was seeing on this bus ride. The clanking metal bridge we just crossed and the motorboats in the water below. I thought, not that long ago, only Indians would be paddling canoes on this wide, clear, quiet Hudson River. I would tell my mother how I could almost *see* what it must have looked like then, without the rusty, iron docks, before the trails of gasoline. She would like that.

I took it all into my mind, like a movie I was watching, and I imagined telling her all about everything, every detail, every comment. I imagined her listening, nodding and approving.

The bus drove through Poughkeepsie. We were definitely in a city now. I kept my focus out the window. Maybe I'd forget I didn't belong here. Maybe something would look familiar.

After all, we used to live around here, on the other side of the river, before my mom and dad got divorced. We lived in New Paltz, where I live now. Again. But we had only lived there one year, and I can hardly remember it at all. After the divorce, my mom and I moved to Woodstock. A year later we moved to Phoenicia. We only stayed there for a year. And then we moved to Shandaken. I went to three different schools in less than three years.

But it's my house in Shandaken that I miss the most. I dream about it. In my dream, I am walking around from room to room and everything is gone. The whole house is empty. It almost looks as if the windows and doors are missing, like one of those open-sided dollhouses. The walls are bare. The furniture and rugs and paintings are all gone, and the wallpaper is peeling, like it's been abandoned for years. When I wake up, I have this terrible feeling. It takes me a long time to shake it. Sometimes all morning.

That's not really what the house looked like when we lived there. It was full and warm. In the summer it seemed to grow right out of all the wild, thorny plants and bushes that surrounded it. In the winter, the wood-stove poured out so much heat that we had to open the windows a little bit and let the frosty air in from outside. Then it would get too cold and we'd shut the windows again. By morning the stove had gone out, and it was just freezing. Freezing.

There were wide slate steps that led right up to the front door from the road below. You had to walk under a splintery, white wooden arch, so dripping with vines you had to push them away to walk through. The steps were steep and they wobbled if you didn't walk right up the center. The first step was cracked in half and the last step was almost completely missing.

We rented the house. There were only a couple of other houses on the road, but nobody lived in those houses in the winter the way we did. The kitchen had a backdoor and a wooden screen door that banged shut behind you. It led out to a little flat spot with dirt and some grass, and then up to the garden and our well, which was just a really deep hole in the ground covered by a piece of wire mesh. You could peer down into the darkness and hear the water rushing far below. You could drop a pebble in and listen for the splash. Then farther up were the woods, which seemed to lead out to the rest of the world.

To history.

Or maybe that's just the way I remember it.

Maybe because I always used to pretend I was a pioneer. Sometimes, I played by myself, but most of the time Anne came with me, even though she was five years younger. If she found me, she followed — and I usually let her find me.

We would walk up into the woods where there was nothing, nothing to remind us that it wasn't the olden days. There was even a mossy, stone wall winding around the trees and along the edges of hills. Somebody long ago had built that wall, stone by stone. We walked for miles like that, pretending we lived a hundred years ago. Playing.

We didn't play the way boys play, running around chasing each other, making shooting noises. It was more like walking, just walking and talking and making up our lives and adventures.

But when it was too cold out, or raining, or when we were just bored with the olden days, we played Little People. We played Little People with armless, legless

Fisher-Price toys, miniature figures, even those plastic trolls with the big ears and bulging eyes. We played with anything and everything we had — blocks and books, shoe boxes, and toy cars.

We played until playing became more real than real was. And better, of course.

Chapter Two

"Want me to open your window?"

I turned around in my seat.

"Huh?" I said to the voice that had brought me back to the school bus, and this field trip, and living with my dad again. And Gail.

"It's hot," a boy said. "I thought you'd want your window open. Well, I mean I saw you trying to open it before."

I think I knew this boy was in sixth grade, like I was. I must have seen him before in the hall or something, but I never noticed that he was really tall. He was standing up in the aisle right next to me. Any minute the teacher would be yelling for him to sit down. Maybe yelling at me, too, for no reason.

But it was September and it was hot. My window was stuck shut, and I was sweating.

"Thanks," I said. I slid back and pressed myself flat against my seat.

The boy stretched over me to reach the window. I slouched down to be out of the way. His whole body was right in my face. The top of my head was practically touching the armpits of his shirt. I slid down further and shut my eyes until I heard the window drop open.

Then I heard him sit down beside me.

I kept my eyes down, and I opened them slowly. I saw his knees right next to mine. I saw his big feet and then his socks, which were bright orange, and it looked like he was staying.

"You don't remember me, do you?" he asked.

"No," I answered. Though now I was close enough to get a good look at his face. He had dark hair, and darkish, olive-y skin, and a thin shadow of what must've been dark hair just above his lip. I looked away.

"Will Hiller?" he tried. "From second grade?"

"Sorry," I added, and I lifted my eyes to see his reaction.

He looked kind of hurt. Or disappointed maybe. I felt sorry, but he was probably thinking of someone else he remembered from second grade. Any minute he was going to realize that, and we'd both be embarrassed. Me especially. He would get up from this seat really quick, and that would be that.

But he didn't get up.

"Should I?" I asked. "Remember you, I mean."

"Well, we were in Miss Greiger's class. Remember?"

And then as he said it, I suddenly did. I remembered Miss Greiger.

Miss Greiger was a very big woman. She wore big dresses. She had a really pretty face, and she was so nice. She left in the middle of the year for two weeks, and when she came back she was *Mrs.* Greiger. She wrote the word COINCIDENCE on the board in white chalk and gave everybody five minutes to come up with as many words as they could using the letters in the word *coincidence*. I think it was supposed to be fun.

I was not a good speller. But I liked Miss/Mrs. Greiger a lot, and one of these days I hoped she would notice me. I wanted her to like me, and maybe she would if I could be one of the winners of this game. If only I could come up with the most words.

But I got so nervous that when she said "go," it was all over before I could really get started. I didn't come up with more than five or six words before the time ran out. I remember I suddenly felt like crying, and I remember I was surprised that I felt like crying.

I moved away before the end of that year with my

mother, so it didn't matter if Miss/Mrs. Greiger ever got to like me or not.

"Yeah, I remember her. I didn't like her," I told Will Hiller. But I did like her. I liked her so much. I kept looking out the window.

"I mean, she didn't like me," I said. I could see my face reflected in the glass.

"*I* liked you," Will said.

Now I *knew* he was thinking of somebody else.

"You don't really remember me," I said.

"Yes, I do. You just don't remember me. I remember when we were getting our class picture taken in the library. We were all standing on these bleachers, and the photography guy told everybody to smile. But you wouldn't."

I had to grin thinking about that. It sounded like something I would do.

"At first he was really nice and made jokes and everything, but you wouldn't smile," Will said. "Then he started to get mad, and the teacher told you to cooperate. And then she said that if you didn't smile immediately, she was going to have to remove you from the bleachers."

I started to laugh. I think it was the first time since school started — no, since summer ended — that I had laughed. Since I moved here with my dad. Or maybe since even before I left for camp.

"I did? She did? She *said* that?" I asked Will.

He nodded. "Yeah, but you pressed you lips together, and you made this face." Will pressed his lips tightly together, squinted his brows, and slid his eyes from side to side.

Yup, that was me. It was my face. My mean face. I would shift my eyes from side to side, back and forth when I was mad, or when someone was lecturing me, or when I was getting in trouble (and someone was *often* lecturing me, and I got in trouble *a lot*).

But when my dad talked about my mean face, it sounded funny. Like he thought it was cute or something. My dad even had this little song about me.

There was a little girl.
Who had a little curl
right in the middle of her forehead.
And when she was good,
She was very very good.
And when she was bad, she was horrid.

"So what happened?" I asked Will.

"You never smiled," Will said. "The guy had to take the picture anyway, and by that time a couple kids were sitting down, and one kid was picking his nose. It's in the picture. Don't you have one?"

"No, I don't think I ever got a class picture. I moved away before the end of the year. My parents got divorced."

"Oh," Will said quietly. "So . . . why are you back now? Here?"

Why was I back.

I turned to look out the window again. We were pulling into the gates of the Roosevelt Mansion. There were huge, old trees lining the long entrance, branches bending, showing the way. Ahead I could see red shutters and a stone roof. I could even see sparkling rays of morning sun. It must be the river again, behind the house, reflecting the light.

"I'm living with my dad now," I said. And then I added quickly, "But only for a little while. Until my mom comes back for me. She's getting us settled in California."

I was lying.

"Then she's going to send for me," I lied again.

"Wow," Will said. "California. That's cool."

The bus lurched to a stop, and before the teachers could say anything, everybody was standing up in the aisle and heading forward.

"Stop!" one of the teachers shouted.

My teacher, Mrs. Thomsen, didn't say anything. She stood up by the door with her clipboard. I guess she's not so bad. At least she doesn't yell.

"Everybody sit back down and wait," the other teacher shouted again.

Only a few kids listened.

It was getting hot again without the breeze from outside and with all the standing bodies crowding around us. Kids were talking and pushing against each other. Pairing up. Complaining.

"Oh well, that's too bad," Will said. He and I were still sitting.

"What?" I asked.

"What what?"

"What you just said . . ." I asked again, "What's too bad?"

The doors were finally opened, and the bodies moved forward and down the steps. The other teacher was still yelling.

"It's too bad you're moving to California," Will said. We both stood up and began shuffling toward the front of the bus.

Mrs. Thomsen was counting heads out loud as we passed. I could barely hear Will talking.

"What did you say?" I asked. Will was behind me.

He answered me. "I wish you were staying," he said. "That's all."

We got put into different groups because Will had the other language arts teacher, the one who was not Mrs. Thomsen. I waved to Will.

"Save me a seat on the way back," Will shouted. I said I would.

For the first time in a really long time, I had something to look forward to. I was looking forward to the bus ride back to school.

Dear Mom,

This is not going to be a long letter like my other ones. Just a quick note because I'm so tired today.

We went on a field trip to Roosevelt Mansion where one of those President Roosevelts lived, I guess. I think you would have liked it because there was a lot of old stuff around and old photos and antiques. There was even a little silver brush and a mirror and a box of powder with <u>real</u> powder in it, like someone had put it there just the night before, rolled over, and gone to sleep. And a little pair of wire glasses, leaning on a tiny, red book.

It gave me a headache though. The bus ride was really hot and most of the kids were singing that dumb beer song all the way back to school. My teacher is pretty nice though. Her name is Mrs. Thomsen and there was one kid who was nice to me. He said he remembers me from second grade. Can you believe that? I can hardly remember <u>myself</u> from second grade. I don't think I believe him. Maybe he just didn't have anyone else to sit with.

Anyway, how can I trust anyone who wears orange socks? Really. Orange. But he's okay. He's pretty nice actually. I think you'd like him.

Other than that I really don't like it here. Besides Gail is driving me crazy. She is so different than you. She thinks she's Martha Stewart or something. She's so fussy about her house. She is really mean to me and Dad doesn't even notice anything, as usual. Maybe I should call his office and make an appointment. Ha Ha.

Well, I really miss you and I love you so much and sometimes this really weird thing happens to me here. Sometimes I wake up from a dream in the morning and I think I am still home. With you. It takes me a while to figure it all out again. Sometimes it takes me the whole morning, till I'm dressed and had breakfast and I'm on the bus.

I really miss you.

I can't wait to see you. Oh, and wait till you see me again. I'm pretty tall now. At camp there was only one little rectangle mirror over the sink in the girl's bathroom. You had to stand on the toilet to see your whole body in it, but then you couldn't see your head. And someone had to be holding the stall door open besides. It was hard to really see your whole self. But when I got here, Gail had this big stand-up mirror in her room. I wouldn't normally ever go in there, but one day, when she was out all day for a big shopping all the way in Poughkeepsie, I snuck in.

I could see I had gotten pretty tall. I must have grown a lot over the summer, like two inches maybe. But I look kind of funny really. Like my body is too big for my head. Like one of those pictures in that stages of puberty hand-out (except that I would never stand there naked like that!) I look like the one in the middle kind of. I look older than I am, I think. Older than I feel, at least. But different. I am really different, even if nobody else can tell.

Boy, that was a pretty long letter after all. I always did talk too much.

love, Leah

Chapter Three

"So how was school today?"

This was obviously Gail talking, because my dad would never say anything like that. My dad is a clinical psychologist, which means he talks to people all day and helps them with their problems, and then by the time he gets home he is mostly all done listening.

Except if he's trying to fix someone or something. Then he's got plenty to say and plenty of big words to say it with. But he doesn't listen. He just talks.

We were all sitting at the dinner table, me and Gail and my dad. Gail insisted that we eat as a family, which I thought was stupid since I had more of a family when I lived with my mom, and we never sat at a table. Sometimes we ate in the living room, reading a book. Or we ate outside in the grass when it was nice enough. Lots of times we ate in the car while we were driving. If my mom wasn't home I just ate in bed.

Sitting at a dinner table doesn't make you a family. It doesn't make this my home.

Gail asked me again. "Leah, so how was school?"

She wasn't going to let this go, was she? I thought.

The trick is not to answer directly but not to appear totally defiant and get in trouble, either. The trick is to hold on to what power you have while appearing to answer the question.

"Hmmm," I mumbled.

The problem is Gail never gives up. It's like she just has to win.

"Does *hmmm* mean it was a good day?" Gail asked.

"Not really," I said. This was already more than I had intended on giving up. I hated school, but I didn't want Gail or my father to know this. I didn't want my father to worry about me. He might have appeared disinterested, but he took everything really seriously. Because then he'd have something to fix. And oh boy, if my dad thought you had a problem, you *really* had a problem, because he was never going to stop talking.

And I *definitely* didn't want Gail to know how I felt about things. I didn't want her to know I was lonely and sad sometimes, like most of the time. Your enemy should never see you hesitate. The same way you're not supposed to run when a dog is chasing you. Sometimes you just have to stand your ground.

And get bitten.

I should have just said, "fine" to Gail, and that would have been the end of that.

"I mean, I just have a lot of homework," I said quickly.

Now I had said two sentences in a row. I had volunteered information without being asked. I had initiated a sentence. Gail pounced on it.

"Oh, what subject? Maybe I can help?"

The truth is I wasn't sure what homework I had, but I would never want any help with it. Maybe it was language arts homework for Mrs. Thomsen. Maybe it was math homework. (If it was math homework I wasn't going to do it, anyway.)

I had been in school here for a little over a month, but already I could tell I wasn't doing very well. Mostly it was because I just didn't do my homework, but I didn't *not* do it on purpose.

Sometimes it was hard enough just getting up, figuring out what to wear, how not to stand out, and how not to look like I was trying to blend in. Who to talk to and who not to talk to. Where to sit and where to hide. That took up a lot of energy. Sometimes when I did my homework, it was so bad, I just didn't turn it in. Most times I just forgot.

I don't know.

But I didn't do very well on that spelling test last week, either. And when I went next door for science and math I knew the teacher, Mr. Kelly, didn't like me at all. He had already sent home a note saying I had a bad attitude. He said I was negative and *blasé*.

Blasé — with an accent — and he had to draw the accent in with a pen because it was a typewritten note. That takes a lot of effort for a teacher.

Blasé doesn't even sound that bad, but it probably is.

My dad read the note and started twiddling a pencil in and out of his fingers. He looked like he was going to say something serious to me. I was just getting ready to start shifting my eyes back and forth and wrinkle my forehead when suddenly my dad reached out and just rubbed the top of my hair, like I was a naughty puppy or something.

He told me to try a little harder, "But don't worry about it. Okay?"

It was so obvious. He was doing "the paradox" on me. The paradox is when you say exactly the opposite of what you want the person to do, hoping that they will then do what you wanted them to do in the first place.

As if now I would start focusing on my schoolwork and try harder.

Yeah, right.

Gail was still waiting for me to respond to her homework help offer.

"No," I said. "I can do it myself."

"Oh," Gail said.

I stood up quickly with my plate and cup before Gail could try and make me say "No *thank you*," and I went into the kitchen.

I put my dishes in the sink and I stared at the soapy water.

When I lived in Shandaken I used to wash the dishes all the time. I played with the forks and spoons and knives in the warm water. The forks were the princesses and the knives were the princes. And all the spoons were always little kids. The princesses would need saving. The knives would have to fight. And the little kids needed to be protected.

"Leah?" My dad said. He came up behind me with his plate. He let it slip into the soapy suds, right next to mine.

"Yeah?" I said. I kept rinsing my plate with this long, scrubby brush thingy that Gail made us use.

"You know I'm trying to work things out," he began. "I told you about the hearing. And the lawyer ―"

"I'm fine, Dad," I interrupted him. This brush thingy was hollow inside and filled with green dish detergent that came out when you squeezed it. "I just don't need any help with my homework. I don't even have any tonight."

"You said you had a lot," he said.

"I don't," I said. I was thinking that my mother would never even *think* to buy something as dumb as this dishwasher brush.

My dad rubbed his hand on my back. "I'm always here, you know," he said. "If you want to talk. You know that, right?"

I arched my back a little, just a little, just an inch, so his hand would slip away.

"Yeah, Dad," I said. "I know." I felt his hand slip away, and I wondered if my dad felt it, too.

He kissed the top of my head and went back into the dining room with Gail. I could hear them talking softly. As I was heading out of the kitchen I saw the tip of a white bag sticking out of a bowl. The bowl was on the top shelf of the cabinet, and the cabinet door was slightly open.

I just knew what was up there. It took me two seconds to climb up on the counter. I turned toward the cabinet and quietly opened it. I reached for the white paper bag and pulled it out.

I was right.

Inside was a package of Hershey's Kisses. I love Hershey's Kisses.

I thought I would just take a handful or so, but when I lifted it out to take a few, I saw the bag hadn't been opened yet.

If I tore it open and took some, Gail would notice for

sure. She'd know that it hadn't been opened. But if I took the whole thing, maybe she'd forget it was there. Or she'd think she put it somewhere else. She'd think she forgot where she put it, and by the time she looked for it, she'd forget the whole thing. Then maybe she'd just buy another bag.

I carefully stepped down off the counter with the white paper bag and the Hershey's package inside, and I slipped quietly to my room.

Chapter Four

It seems like a million years ago but it was just of couple of months, the end of last summer, my dad came to pick me up from camp.

I was expecting my mom.

I should have known something was wrong weeks before, but I was too dumb. You wouldn't think a person could be so dumb, but I am living proof. I should have known my mother wasn't coming to get me, because she never answered any of my letters from camp. But like I said, I was too dumb.

Everyone at camp had to write home. They made you do it. Once a week, sometimes more, the older counselors barred the doors of our cabins and told us to take out paper and pencil. And to take out money if you didn't have self-addressed stamped envelopes, like Joanie Miller did.

I didn't need any coercing. I always wrote to my mother, and I told her everything. I hadn't really wanted to go to camp in the first place, but now that I was here — a lot had happened. Mostly, that I had kissed a boy. Or rather I had been kissed by a boy while playing spin the bottle. It was dark. We were all sitting cross-legged in the broom closet of the mess hall. The spinning bottle pointed to me.

And I was kissed.

It was mushy and kind of wet-lipped. I just sat there and didn't move.

I just knew there had to be more to this than *this*. I didn't even know the boy's name. I'm sure he didn't know mine.

This was pretty awful.

Really awful.

I can't really figure out why I did it.

I also shaved my legs for the first time. The girl in the bunk above me said she had been shaving for three years already. (That would place her actual first shave at age eight. I think she was lying, but who am I to say anything?) She showed me how to do it, but she only let me do one little spot because she didn't want me to use up her only Pink Lady Razor on my whole leg, let alone on both. So one straight run, only halfway right up the back of my left calf. The skin was left smooth and soft and bald of dark hair. I loved it, but it grew back really fast.

And I wrote all about it in my next letter home.

Mail that arrived for the campers was handed out in the evening, in the mess hall, after singing time. I learned a lot of new songs. "The Ship Titanic." "Who Built the Ark?" "An Old Austrian Went Climbing on a Mountaintop High." But I never got any letters back from my mother.

My dad wrote a few times. About once a week. He wrote to me about the weather, his new office. He sent me a care package with shampoo and batteries and candy, but he never let on that anything had changed — that my whole life had changed. I didn't find out until the last of camp, the day he came to pick me up.

"Leah, I have to tell you something," he began. His eyes were focused on the road in front of him. Sleep-away camp was two states, hundreds of miles, and three hours behind us. My sleeping bag and duffel bag were stuffed into the trunk of the car, along with a macramé plant hanger, two découpage hot plates, a woodcut of my name, and five lopsided lanyard key chains.

"You're going to be living with me now. And Gail," my dad said.

Nothing after that moment seemed real. I was crying so hard I couldn't see out of my eyes. I couldn't breathe. I couldn't think. I couldn't believe it, but I knew it was true almost immediately. We were driving to my dad's house in New Paltz, where I had visited him on weekends, where he lived with Gail since they've been married.

Not home to Shandaken.

"You can pick which room you want, Leah," my dad said. "We cleared out Gail's sewing room and the guest room. Either one."

I was still crying.

"Honey, it's better this way," my dad said.

"Where is she?" I choked.

"She's moved."

"Where?"

"Leah, please . . ."

"Where, tell me. Where did she go?"

"California," he said.

He started to tell me something about Anne, about lawyers, and about a hearing, but I was underwater, under pounds of pressure, water clogging my ears and pouring out of my face.

We had another hour to drive. I cried the whole way.

"Everything's going to be fine," my dad said, as we pulled into the driveway.

I hope he has better advice for people who pay him.

Chapter Five

So I picked the room with the sun shining in through all the windows. There were windows on three of the walls. I chose it because brightness was all I could see. My dad started bringing in my furniture from my room in Shandaken, before I had even put down my backpack. He carried in my rolltop desk and the little chair that fit right under it. He carried in my bed, too. He set it on its side, in four pieces. My pillow, my sheets, and my blankets from home were all there, folded in a pile.

Then my dad dragged in my bureau. He pushed it against the far wall, opposite the double window. He was sweating by this point but still smiling, which was not like him, at all. He set up my bed in record time.

"Okay, sweetie?" he asked.

Then he went back out to the car for my duffel bag and my découpage before I could answer.

I walked over to my bureau. I touched it as if to see that it was real. It was the same bureau. It *was* mine. I opened the drawers, and my clothes were inside as if nothing had happened. They were laying there, as stupid as I was.

"Here you go," my dad said, walking in again. He dropped my heavy bag down on the floor.

"Why don't you take everything out, and we can wash it all. It's probably pretty dirty from a month at camp," he said. He smiled, sort of.

I looked at my dad. He was my dad, but nothing made sense.

"Is this everything?" I asked.

My dad nodded. He wiped his brow with his untucked shirt. He looked as though he had just accomplished something big and important, so I didn't ask again.

I didn't say anything then, and I never have.

I knew, just as I knew my mother wasn't coming to get me, that everything was gone. My jewelry box, my CDs, my stuffed animals. My toys, (even though I hadn't played with them in a long time), two puzzles, my rock collection. My collection of flattened pennies (I had five of them). My scrapbook (it was empty, but I was planning on using it one day). My Francie Doll, still in the box (because I never had much use for Barbies). And my books.

All my books. I had Nancy Drew and Harry Potter

books and *Misty of Chincoteague*. I had five Little House on the Prairie books. I had six American Girl books. *All-of-A-Kind-Family*. Two of the real Wizard of Oz books, *Ozma of Oz* and *Tic Toc of Oz*. *Belle Prater's Boy* and *Memories of Summer*. I had all three E. B. White books. They were all gone.

"Okay, Dad," I said. I sat on the floor and acted as if I was going to open my duffel and take out all the dirty clothes, white and dark, for the laundry. Because that's what he wanted me to do.

"Okay," he said. I didn't look up, but I knew he wasn't budging. He was just standing there.

"I'm fine, now," I said.

"I know you are," he said, because he wanted me to be.

After he left, I stood up and walked back over to my bureau. On top was a long table runner of pink and white lace, just as I had left it back home in Shandaken.

It had been a gift. My mother had given it to me. I remember, she said it would look just perfect in my room — on my bureau — and it had. It looked perfect there.

And as I was thinking of it, I could almost feel the memory of her gift fading from my mind. Had it been a birthday gift or just a thought? Did she give it to me last year or the year before? Was I with her when she bought it, or did she come home with it and lay it on this bureau as a surprise?

I couldn't exactly remember.

I knew I had to do something.

I carefully slipped the lace off the top of my bureau and folded it, once and then again. I opened my top drawer and slipped the folded lace deep inside, far against the back wood of the bureau and under all my clothes. It would be safe there. It wouldn't get lost or ruined. It wouldn't fade from the sun that was going to pour in these windows tomorrow morning, and the morning after that, and the one after that.

Dear Mom,

I know you wouldn't want me eating candy and stuff like that but I can't help myself. They have so much here. And Gail likes to bake and cook a lot. You won't believe this one — Gail makes her own mayonnaise and it's awful. Really awful. Why would someone do that? She makes her own spaghetti sauce, too, from real tomatoes. Her spaghetti sauce isn't _as_ bad as the mayonnaise, but I have to eat around all these big chunks of tomato skins and long stringy onions. I have to pick them out and leave them on the side of my plate, even though I know Gail is watching me and doesn't like when I do that.

She thinks it's rude.

That's why I do it.

Maybe you are right about the junk food. I just

ate a whole half a bag of Hershey Chocolate Kisses that were laying around in the kitchen, so I can't do my reading homework. I was going to do it but now I kind of have a bad stomachache.

You would like my language arts teacher, I think. She reads a lot. She has <u>A Wrinkle in Time</u> on her desk. Wasn't that one of your favorites when you were little?

Well, I better go to sleep now. I have to get up really early here to catch the bus. But at least it comes right to the door. Remember how I always missed the bus in Shandaken because it was so far to walk? And then we all just stayed home.

I miss you so much. More than you can imagine.

love, Leah

Chapter Six

Gail was in the kitchen. Cooking. Cooking cookies, I think. And she was wearing an apron. Baking, I guess then. She was baking cookies.

I never saw anyone wear a real apron before, except on TV. But Gail really wears one. It's white, flouncy around the bottom and the arm holes. I bet my mother would think it was hilarious.

"Wanna help?" Gail was asking me.

"No," I said, and as soon as it came out, I realized it had sounded more nasty than I meant it to. I mean, I meant to say "no" but maybe not like *No way. Are you kidding?*

Gail just smiled and kind of shrugged, like it didn't bother her. She must have been taking paradox lessons from my dad. But she didn't fool me.

"What are you making, anyway?" I asked.

I got a little flour on my sleeve as I leaned on the counter. Everything was out all over the kitchen. The bag of flour and sugar, a tiny dark bottle of something, little spoons and big spoons, and bowls, and the milk, and little packets, and two measuring cups — one metal and one glass. There was a messy, full feeling in the room. The oven was heating the air.

"Drop sugar cookies," Gail said. She had one finger holding open a page in her cookbook. Index cards stuck out of the other pages. All stained. Old stains. "And banana bread."

"Two things?" I asked. "You're making two things at the same time?"

Gail laughed. "I might as well," she said. "Don't you think?"

That's when my stomach betrayed me with a low gurgle. I shifted around with my feet to cover up the sound, but it was too late.

"The first batch of cookies is ready," Gail said. "Try one?"

I couldn't very well say I wasn't hungry.

"I guess so," I said, shrugging and taking a bite.

It was the best cookie I had ever tasted. It was warm and sweet, but not too sweet. And then there was a surprise. Inside was a tiny bit of melted chocolate, like a hidden message. Only a tiny taste.

Gail handed me another one. I took it and Gail smiled.

"Thank you," I said. I didn't think about it. It just came out, just like that — *thank you.*

I didn't want to leave that sentence alone in the air too long. I didn't want anyone getting too used to the sound of it, start expecting it or anything.

"So did you used to be a baker or something?" I asked Gail quickly.

She laughed again. "No, I was a lawyer or something."

Gail was a lawyer. I couldn't picture it. Not at all. She didn't seem like a lawyer. She just seemed like a Gail, like a baker-sewing-nagging kind of woman. But then again I didn't think much about Gail, really. I didn't think much about what she did, or what she used to do, or what she felt.

"Well, I still am a lawyer," Gail was going on. "I mean, one day . . . I might look for a job around here."

But I wasn't really listening. I was still thinking about how hard it is to think about someone else when you're spending most of your time worrying about yourself. That thought, for some reason, made me thirsty. I got myself some milk from the fridge.

There are some things you can't eat without a glass of milk. Like peanut butter and jelly. You can't have peanut butter and jelly without milk. Or cookies.

"In fact, yesterday I was over in Poughkeepsie and . . ." Gail was talking.

And then all at once it seemed so obvious. Gail didn't

marry my dad expecting to have me living with them. I'm sure I didn't fit into her picture of what it was to get married, buy a house, and be a big lawyer lady.

I was a mistake. I didn't belong in this picture.

Gail must have noticed I wasn't paying attention. She was quiet, maybe she was thinking the exact same thing. She started taking things out of the fridge for dinner and putting them on the counter.

"Leah, you know I'm in the kitchen anyway . . ." she started. "If you want me to make your lunch for school. I'd be happy . . . I mean, I could just do it the night before and leave it here in the refrigerator."

Maybe, it would have been really nice to have Gail make my lunch. But I would never ask. I didn't belong here, and neither would my lunch.

"No," I blurted out.

If the air in the room had been colored, you would have seen it change — blue to red, or white to black. And if you couldn't see it, you would have felt it.

"No, thank you." Gail said. She didn't turn around. She had her head in the fridge again. But I could hear her perfectly.

At first, I was confused. Why was Gail saying "no, thank you" to me? For a second, I thought I had done something nice, but I knew I hadn't. Then I realized Gail was trying to get *me* to say "No, thank you" to *her*.

But I knew I wouldn't.

Chapter Seven

I regretted that "no" for two reasons. Maybe three reasons. One, was because I felt bad right away and could barely choke down my last cookie. And two, in the long run, I probably would have liked to eat a bag lunch much better. But mostly, three, because I now have to stand at the end of the cafeteria line holding my tray and looking like a total jerk, trying to figure out where I can sit.

If I had a bag lunch I could have slipped in quicker and found a nice quiet seat somewhere. There are rows of big long tables, and every table seems to have permanent occupants. Boys, girls, brains, cheerleaders, jocks, skateboarders, preppies, grunge, losers.

I suppose I have to sit at the loser table again.

The losers all sit at the same table but not together. Some cluster down at the end. One or two in the middle.

They pretend they don't know they are at the loser table, like it's some temporary situation or something. But once you sit down there, chances are you'll never sit anywhere else.

My eyes moved around the room. I saw Will Hiller waving at me.

I mean, I thought he was waving at me. Maybe he was waving at the person behind me, and if I waved back I'd look like an idiot. My tray was getting really heavy. If someone bumped into me and I dropped this tray I'd be a bigger idiot, and I would probably die of embarrassment. Every minute that I stood here my chances of that happening increased exponentially.

I looked back over to Will. He was still waving. I turned around quickly. There *was* no one behind me.

"Yeah, you," Will must have said. I could see his lips moving.

I headed over.

Will wasn't at the loser table. He wasn't even at a table. He was sitting on a wide ledge that stuck out from the wall by the window. His tray was balanced on the lost-and-found shelves next to him.

"They let you sit here?" I asked. I propped my feet up on the bottom shelf and rested my tray on top. It was actually very comfortable and best of all, it was out of the way, a whole separate category.

"Yeah," Will said. "The good thing about being different is that kids leave you alone. And teachers are happy if other kids just leave you alone. So they let me sit here."

"I'm different, too!" I practically shouted.

God, did that sound stupid.

For some reason I do that a lot. When someone says something about themselves, I seem destined to blurt out that I do it, too. Or I like that, too. Or I have one just like that. It's so dumb, but it comes out before I can stop it.

But Will didn't seem to notice.

"Yeah, so you can sit here, too," he said. He smiled at me.

He had braces that I didn't notice before, when we were on the bus. And he had on the same big, green sneakers, the kind basketball players used to wear in those days when they wore those little shorty shorts like you see on ESPN Classic. He had dark brown eyes with long black eyelashes. He didn't look like anyone I had ever known before, like any boy. So he was different, and he seemed to like it that way.

And, well, he was cute — handsome — I guess that's the only way to put it.

Will scooted over so I could have the wider perch, closest to the shelf I put my tray on.

And he was nice.

"Thanks," I said.

"Sure thing."

I tried to take tiny bites of my macaroni and cheese, one macaroni at a time. But I was hungry, and then I was almost done. I finished my applesauce, too. I was working on my cake. Eating is not the most attractive thing you can do in front of a boy. Besides, Will ate really fast. I didn't want to be left behind.

"Do you have Mr. Lennox for math?" Will asked.

"No, I have the other guy. Mr. Kelly?"

"Oh, right, but we use the same book," Will answered. "Did you do the homework?"

"No, did you?"

Will was long done eating. He was breaking off the ends of his plastic fork. "Well, my tutor did it with me," Will said. "So at least I know I've got all the answers right."

I wasn't sure if a tutor was a good thing or a bad thing by the way Will said that.

"Why do you have a tutor?" I asked.

"My parents tell me I have to have a tutor because they 'care about me so much'," Will said. "Isn't that crazy? I hate having a tutor. Well, I like the tutor, but I hate that I have to have one. But I can give you the math answers if you want."

Will slid off his perch with his tray balanced in his hands. He kept talking as I followed him to the little window in the wall where you throw everything out and return your tray. Except we have these cardboard trays, and you're just supposed to throw them away, too.

"My parents try harder because I'm adopted, I think. I

mean, I know I'm adopted, but it's my theory that they think they have to try harder. It's like if I'm not smart, they can't blame it on Uncle Charlie or Grandma Molly's dumb genes. Right? So they try harder. So, do you want the math answers?"

I had never met anyone who was adopted before. At least, not that I knew of.

"Well, it might look kind of suspicious if I get all the answers right for the first time," I said slowly.

"Well, just copy some right and some wrong," Will said. "That's what I do."

"It might look kind of suspicious if I have *any* of the answers right," I said.

Will laughed. His smile went right up to his eyes.

I was wondering if his mother had given him away when he was first born, or whether she had died. Or was it later, when his mother decided she didn't want him anymore. Like me. I agreed to take the math answers.

Then, Will turned to me and said, "Instead of going outside wanna do something else?"

"Like what?" I asked casually. Though, I would have done almost anything else than go out for recess. Being outside was just another territorial negotiation I dreaded.

"Well, I'll show you, but you can't tell anyone."

I was following him already.

"It's nothing bad," Will went on. "I just don't really

like going outside. There's nothing to do. And nobody to do it with." He smiled.

"Yeah, I know," I said. "And yeah, I promise."

Together we silently crept down the hall right past the cafeteria ladies and the teachers' room. Wherever we were going it had to be better than going out for recess.

Yesterday on the playground, two girls ran over to me and rubbed leaves in my hair.

Chapter Eight

"What's the matter?" Will asked me.

I was standing just inside the auditorium. The light disappeared as the tall, wide doors pressed shut behind us.

"It's dark in here," I said.

"You've got to get used to it," Will said. He started down the center aisle. He ran, kind of skipped all the way. Then he hopped up onto the stage in one graceful jump.

A little light seeped in around the doors, but I stood at the top of the aisle until my eyes could adjust. Will was already walking across the stage. He was doing something up there. I squinted my eyes but I couldn't figure it out. The lights above each exit were beginning to spread a red glow. I could see a little bit.

Will was pretending. He was playing.

I recognized it right away. After all, it wasn't that long ago that I used to do that all the time.

❧❧❧

RAILROAD TRACKS ran beside our house in Shandaken. I had flattened my five pennies there. Below the tracks was the Esopus Creek. Sometimes Anne and I wandered all the way up through the woods and down the other side to the banks to the creek. In the spring, waters from melted snow ran full and wild into creek. It became a raging river with deep dips and turns and whirlpools racing around massive rocks. Truckloads of teenagers parked up on Route 28, their flatbeds piled with inner tubes. They would race down to the creek with tires on their arms and jump into the rushing water. All you could see were their arms and legs sticking out over the side as they swirled away downstream, sometimes with a can in one hand.

They would be shouting and laughing, but you couldn't hear them, their mouths moving in a silent movie. All you could hear was the water, pouring over rocks, speeding away. Deafening and thrilling.

But by late summer everything got quiet. The water in the creek was so low that huge boulders stuck out from mucky mud. Little pools of smelly, fishy water were all that was left. When the water was low like that, Anne and I could walk along right down the center of the

43

creek from rock to slimy rock. Heat rose up from the ground in waves. All we could hear were the cicadas buzzing in the trees. The teenagers were gone.

Anne and I could pretend to be whoever we wanted to be. We played.

"Who am I?" Anne would insist.

"You're an indentured servant who was sent to America from England to work for a farmer. But the farmer was so cruel you had to run away. You lived for three weeks in the forest, eating bugs —"

"Eww," Anne said.

"But then you were discovered by an Iroquois Indian tribe and nursed back to health," I said.

"I was sick?"

"What do you think happens when you eat bugs?"

"The Indians took care of me?"

"Yeah. They spoon-fed you warm corn chowder and buffalo milk. (I realized I was getting my Native-American tribes mixed up, but I didn't let on.)

Anne looked at me. "So I get better?"

"Not yet. First you get sicker."

"I do?"

"Yeah, so they put corn stalks soaked in deer poop and tobacco on your forehead," I told her. (I made that up on the spot.)

"That makes me better?"

"Yeah, it sucks the fever right out of your head."

"Doesn't it smell bad?"

"Deer poop doesn't smell, dummy. Deer are vege-
tarians."

Anne seemed content.

It was hot, and the sun beat down on our backs. I had
lost my bonnet and my petticoats miles ago. I would
soon be adopted by a kind, middle-aged Indian woman
who was in deep in mourning for the loss of her real
daughter. This kind Indian woman had been weeping for
months and months, until she heard that she would have
a new daughter.

That would be — me.

And once I was accepted into the tribe there would be
nothing, absolutely nothing that would make me different than her Indian daughter. She would love me with all
her heart. She would stop crying because that is the Indian way. At least, from what I'd read. I read *Indian Cap-
tive: The Story of Mary Jemison.*

I would be her Indian daughter, in all ways, for all
time.

"Are we both living with the same Indians in the same
village?" Anne asked me, and I told her.

Yes.

Yes. And years and years pass and we both would forget our white man's culture. I would come to love the

Indian life and would marry a brave, handsome warrior. Anne would become a medicine woman and save the tribe from a terrible epidemic of yellow fever.

⁂

"WHAT'S THE MATTER?" Will whispered loudly, startling me out of my memories. "Come on up here."

My eyes had adjusted to the darkness. It was as if there had been enough light to see all along. Will was standing with his feet slightly turned out, almost like a dancer. But he was so lopsided. His shirt was coming untucked from his pants, his pants were too big, one cuff was stuck in his sock. His skin was dark, like an Indian brave.

Like my Indian husband.

I felt myself start to blush. I am a major fast blusher. I can feel my own red cheeks right away, and it takes forever to go away. Sometimes, I swear I could fry an egg on my face.

"Up there?" I shouted back, softly . Maybe my face will return to normal by the time I walk all the way down the aisle, really slow.

The emptiness of the auditorium echoed. Every seat was folded up. A heavy, red curtain hung closed in back of the stage. I could smell varnish and dusty velvet. I looked up at the high, high ceiling. There were lights and wires and microphones tied up to the rafters. No one was here, but you could feel the crowd. You could almost imagine the seats filled and lights shining and music swelling. But right now it was silent and mysterious.

It felt like a secret place, a safe place. It reminded me of something passing, like a dream you are just about to forget. If you don't stop it from fading away.

"Come on up," Will said as I got closer. "Let's sing something."

I didn't think he really meant it at first. I almost started to laugh like I thought I should. But I'm glad I didn't, because he meant it.

"C'mon," he said.

"Okay," I said, and I jumped up onto the stage. I banged my knee against the edge, but I pretended it didn't hurt.

Will and I sang "My Country 'Tis of Thee," because for some reason it was the only song I could think of. At first I just barely whispered the words, and then my voice just kind of slipped into Will's and I let it.

Chapter Nine

*T*he second half of my school day was usually worse than the first. Only today it seemed it might be a little better. Instead of picking dried leaves out of my hair, my body was still echoing with the memory of singing with Will. Maybe science wouldn't be so bad after all.

Some of the kids from my language arts class were in science, too. But many were different. And I still couldn't tell most of the boys from the others, especially the ones with the really short haircuts and basketball T-shirts. They all looked alike to me. I got everybody's names mixed up, too. There were three Kates in first period and two Emmas. Or maybe it was the other way around.

So mostly I kept to myself.

Mr. Kelly taught science and math. He was nothing like Mrs. Thomsen, except that they might have been brother and sister. They were both blonde with blue eyes. Basically Mr. Kelly was a skinnier, meaner version of Mrs. Thomsen. His pants hung off his waist and his plaid shirt off his shoulders. The skin on his face kind of drooped off his bones, too. He had a really big forehead. He looked like a scarecrow, so mean no crow would come near.

But here I was.

"Symbiosis," Mr. Kelly was saying. He had his back to the class, and he was writing on the board. He didn't have that nice, perfect, teacher-handwriting. He had chicken scrawl. I mean *crow scrawl.* Ha!

I almost started to laugh out loud.

Will would have thought that was funny. Crow scrawl. I might even tell Will later. And I'll describe how Mr. Kelly looks, and I'll make it funny. Maybe tomorrow. If we go to the auditorium again.

I wished for it. I think I even clasped my hands together.

"There are three forms of symbiosis," Mr. Kelly said, still facing away from the class. "Parasitism." His handwriting was taking a nosedive toward the bottom right corner of the chalkboard. "Commensalism. And mutualism."

Everyone was taking notes in their books as Mr. Kelly went on to explain each type. I was looking around at the projects hanging on the walls. Pictures and graphs. One class had done charts of how many kids took the bus, and how many walked to school, and how many were driven. Another class did a big graph of who celebrated Hanukkah and who had Christmas or Kwanzaa or "Other." There was one kid in the class who was "Other." I wondered if that was the same little girl who left the room every morning when we said the Pledge.

I think that girl's name was Natalie. I heard it was against her religion, so she got to stand out in the hall until we were finished.

When I was in kindergarten I used to think the Pledge ended with "And to the Republic where *Richard* stands." (I was only five.) And I used to wonder where exactly Richard stood.

And then that reminded me that there was a boy named Richard in Mrs. Thomsen's homeroom. Malk, I think. Richard Malk.

"Excuse me? Miss Baer?" It was Mr. Kelly.

I looked up. A couple kids giggled, which always happens when they hear my last name for the first time. It usually wears off pretty quick.

"Huh?" I said.

"Are you paying attention, Miss Baer? Can you tell me which type of symbiosis is demonstrated by the hookworm?"

The hookworm?

Immediately a swoosh of arms shot up in the class, accompanied by the appropriate gasps for air of those who were certain of the answer. But Mr. Kelly wasn't going for it. He was looking right at me.

I could see the three original choices on the board. Normally I would have gone for the longest word since they say that's usually the right answer. But they all looked like pretty long words. I almost considered counting the letters. Parasitism. Too long.

C-o-m-m-.

And then suddenly a loud ringing.

A fire drill. Unbelievable.

As we filed out the door Mr. Kelly was still staring at me as if blasé were written all over my face.

Dear Mom,

I really hate it here. I hate this whole town. I hate the school. I hate this house. Gail got mad at me the other day when I brushed some crumbs off the counter. She said it just got the floor dirty. I was making myself a peanut butter and jelly sandwich. She said I should wipe the crumbs into my hand or just leave them there and she would clean it.

I told her she could sue me if she wanted, since she was a lawyer and everything. Jeez, I was just kidding but she got really, really mad.

I hate everything here, except for Will. Will

showed me how to sneak into the auditorium instead of going out for recess. We've been going for two weeks now. Almost every day.

Will can draw really good, too. Really good. He is an artist. His artwork is always hanging in the hall outside the art room. The art teacher loooves him. I never met anyone before who could do so many things. He can sing and he sounds like someone in a real Broadway show. His voice is clear like that and loud but not because he's shouting. It's just the sound that fills up the air. Will says the auditorium is designed to do that. He says it's called acoustics, but I know it's his voice. It's something special inside him. And when I am singing with Will, it is the most amazing thing. It almost feels like magic, like reaching up to a high spot way above the ground and being caught, and held there.

Will is really strong, too. He can walk on his hands from one end of the stage all the way to the other.

love and miss you, Leah

PS: Remember I told you I got taller? Well, also you'd be so surprised to see how long my hair got over the summer. Remember how I was trying to grow out my bangs? You said it would be hard but it would be worth it. Well, it was hard but I did it and now I can get all my hair back in a ponytail. It's still wavy but the longer it gets the straighter it is. When I take it out, the waves are mostly on the bottom of my hair and the top is flat and shiny, like an ocean. But of course, my hair is not blue. Ha Ha.

I still sneak into Gail's room when she's not home and look at my whole self sometimes. In my underwear, of course. I still look weird and out of proportion but my long hair helps. Sort of.

Chapter Ten

*S*mash.

I distinctly heard breaking china. I'm sure of it.

I was thinking that I might do my homework tonight. For a change. I was just about to get out my binder. In fact, I had just stood up to get my backpack when I heard it. And I knew what it was right away.

It was Gail. She was in the kitchen, and I was all the way in my room.

She had thrown a dish on the ground. On purpose, you can just tell. And she was talking out loud. I didn't know if she wanted me to hear her. My dad wasn't home yet, so she must be talking to me. Or to herself? I could barely hear her words but I could tell that she was crying.

"What did I do?" she was saying. "Why did I ever —"

Smash. Another dish hit the ground. And broke.

It must have been the crumbs on the floor, or maybe the "why don't you sue me" comment.

I stood perfectly still, listening to my own breathing. In and out. Up and down. I could feel my shoulders moving.

"If she wants something, why doesn't she ask for it?"

Then I figured it out with a shudder. *The candy.*

I looked over to my desk, where I had hidden the white paper bag in the bottom drawer under my rulers and left-over-too-small-to-sharpen pencils and nearly dried-up markers. There were thumb tacks stuck right into the bottom of the drawer and a hardened blob of purple paint. And there was the candy. I didn't even eat it all. Most of it had softened and then hardened back up in little mushed blobs. Some of the Kisses were stuck together. I would never eat it now.

So Gail had noticed the missing candy. She didn't forget or buy another bag. I guess I was wrong about that one. But it's just candy. What's the big deal?

Then it got really quiet, and then I could hear Gail sweeping. I could hear broken pieces of plate clanking together. I could hear Gail sniffing.

So was she mad or sad? Was she going to yell at me or just cry like a baby?

I waited in my room as long as I could. I was afraid to even open my door. I suppose I could have done my homework, but I didn't feel like it anymore. I had lost the momentum.

I figured when my dad got home Gail would tell him everything, and then he'd come in here and lecture me. Analyze me. Fix me. And I would look all over the room, back and forth, everywhere but at him. He might even give me some punishment or take something away from me, although that would be difficult. I didn't care about anything. What could he take away?

I waited a really long time, and finally I heard the automatic garage door open. I could see car lights move across my window and then disappear. I heard the side door open and close.

Footsteps. Conversation. The TV went on. The toilet flushed. Footsteps. More conversation.

About half an hour later my dad popped his head in my room and told me it was time for supper. When I went out to eat I half expected to see fragments of broken dishes, maybe a little blood. But there was nothing, and Gail didn't say anything about it the whole night. Her eyes were a little red, but she didn't say one word.

I sure wasn't going to bring it up.

"Finish all your homework?" my dad asked me as I was getting ready for bed.

"All done," I said.

He smiled and kissed me good night on the top of my forehead.

I felt terrible.

Dear Mom,

Just to tell you, Gail is really crazy. She gets all upset about her stupid candy. So she starts breaking her dishes on the floor. Can you believe it? I mean, she loves her dishes. She told me once she bought them from some special place in England or New England or something. And her kitchen is like her whole life.

Anyway, she knows I took the stupid candy but she'll never say anything to me. She didn't even tell Dad. She just cleaned it up and acted like it never happened. She's so weird, don't you think so?

love, Leah

Chapter Eleven

Mrs. Thomsen wasn't going to be too happy with me. I didn't have my homework done again. I didn't even remember what it was until the other kids were handing in theirs.

Then I remembered.

It was a poem. We were supposed to have written a poem at home. We had learned all these different styles in class. That I remembered. We were reading poems by different writers. There were poems stuck up all over the classroom. Some by famous people, some by kids in the class. Some were really long, and some were really short. I liked the short ones better. I could have just written a short one. Even some famous people wrote really short poems.

Sasha Buckley was collecting the homework. She was

two rows and three desks away and heading right this way. She was probably formulating the exact, perfectly mean thing to say when she got to me. Sasha didn't like me from the first day we met. And I didn't like her, based solely on the principle that girls like Sasha never like girls like me.

In fact, had I realized Sasha was one of those girls who never likes girls like me, I might have avoided the whole situation. But it was only the first day of school, and I didn't have time. You can't tell who is who on the first day.

But basically I talk too much.

Sasha was standing by her locker with a bunch of other girls. A *lot* of other girls — so really I should have known better, because I do know that girls like Sasha travel in packs.

Sasha was wearing these really cool pants, with Velcro and zippers. The kind of pants you can unzip the bottom half of the leg and make them into shorts.

I started walking closer. Sasha was showing some girls how the side pocket of the left leg had another little pocket inside. Of course, I didn't know her name was Sasha at this point, but I soon would.

But I had a pair of pants just like that — a coincidence — I had the *exact* same pants. Gail had just bought them for me before school started. Sasha was shutting her locker.

"I have a pair of pants just like that," I blurted out.

I don't know. I just said it. I thought I was being friendly, but had I thought a minute longer I would never have opened my mouth in the first place.

"Like yours," I said, pointing. "I have the exact same pair."

I think I was smiling like a big idiot.

Sasha looked at me, slowly. Everyone got quiet, as if they could tell something mean was going to come out of Sasha's mouth, and they didn't want to miss one syllable.

I stopped smiling but it was too late.

"Ohhh . . . ," Sasha drew it out very deliberately. "You mean they made more than one pair?"

She raised her eyebrow, and she had the tiny hint of a smile on her face.

It took me a full second or two to realize she was making fun of me. When I did, my face, of course, burned red. And that's when I realized Sasha Buckley was one of those girls that doesn't like me. She doesn't like me because she thinks I'm stupid. And silly. She thinks I'm a goody-two-shoes who gets excited over a pair of pants.

There is a Sasha Buckley in every class.

At some point during the past month, Sasha Buckley learned my name, too.

"Don't have your homework again, Leah?" She was standing at my desk saying that really loud on purpose.

"Yeah, I have it," I said.

I looked right into her face, so she could see that I was not weak and silly, and I was certainly not a goody-two-shoes. But if she stood there one more minute, I was going to start to cry.

"It's in my locker," I said.

"Sure it is," Sasha said, and she moved on. She must not have been in the mood. Or Mrs. Thomsen was too close by. Or that big pimple on her forehead was growing into her skull, clogging up the part of her brain that thinks up mean things to say.

That pimple line might have been a good thing to say, but I had thought of it too late. Sasha was already back at her desk.

The story of my life.

As predicted, Mrs. Thomsen wasn't too happy with me. She must have noticed my homework wasn't in with everybody else's. She made me stay when everyone else left for science class next door. She called me over to her desk.

"Leah? You're missing five homework assignments." Mrs. Thomsen said. She had a soft voice.

In a way, Mrs. Thomsen reminded me of Miss/Mrs. Greiger. She wasn't big like that, but she had the same way of speaking. And she was basically nice. She was basically someone you would want to like you — that is, if you were inclined to care about stuff like that.

Which I wasn't.

"I'm going to give you this weekend to turn in your poem. Okay? And then after that, if you don't have it to me by Monday, you're going to have to start missing recess."

A month ago I would have cheered about that; as I said, anything was better than going out for recess. But for the last few weeks I had been going to the auditorium with Will. I didn't want to mess that up now.

"I'll do it," I said quickly.

"You know, Leah, you might be really good at it," Mrs. Thomsen said.

I was watching my feet. I stared down at the spot on my shoe where I had dropped a little taco sauce last week. The stain looked like a wide-open mouth.

"At what?" I asked.

"Writing," Mrs. Thomsen said. "I've seen what you can do in class. You're more than capable."

The mouth on my shoe looked like it was yelling at me: *Don't be such a big dummy. She's being nice.*

"I'll try," I said. I looked up.

Mrs. Thomsen smiled. "Try hard,"she said.

I nodded and hurried out the door for next period.

Chapter Twelve

I didn't like Gary right from the start. He wasn't like other grown-up men I knew. He wasn't *anything* like my father, who wore a shirt and a tie to work and read newspapers. But Gary wasn't like other, younger men I had seen, either. He was sort of outdoorsy like one of those construction workers on the side of the road wearing a helmet or high up in a tree with a chain saw. He wore jeans and plaid flannel shirts. And he was sort of talky, like a teacher. But he had long hair in a ponytail like a hippie from the sixties, only he wasn't like that either. He wasn't the kind who wore peace signs or flowers in his hair, or played the guitar.

Not at all.

And the worst part of it all was that my mother never would have met Gary, if it hadn't been for me. Gary rented a room in my friend Alexandra's house.

Alexandra was my fifth-grade best friend. I figured out pretty quickly that you need a best friend in order to survive a new school. Every year in every different school, I managed to have a best friend, a girl. In third grade, in Woodstock, it was Jody Roth. Then in Phoenicia, it was Nanette Hilligan, like the old television show *Gilligan's Island*, except with an *H*.

I met Alexandra when we moved to Shandaken.

But Alexandra I really, really liked. I would have liked her even if I hadn't been looking for a best friend.

Alexandra was pretty and so skinny, almost breakable-looking. Her hair was red, but not bright orange-red or deep-burnt red. It was red like an autumn leaf, the pale color of the last leaves left on the trees at the end of the season, just before it snows. Her skin was white, covered with freckles the same faded color as her hair.

Alexandra and I used to spend almost every night we could together. Either at my house or hers. We both lived with only our mothers, but while I would visit my dad every other weekend, I don't know if Alexandra had a father. She never mentioned her father. She never went to visit one or anything.

I think that's why we found each other, because of the questions we never asked each other.

Alexandra had a little sister named Beth, who had the same red hair and white skin and nearly as many freckles. I spent lots and lots of nights at their house. Sometimes, Anne slept over, too, and it was all four girls in one big bed. We watched scary movies on TV, or we played board games. We made up radio shows and taped them on a tape recorder. We played make-believe. (But never Little People. That was only for me and Anne.)

I didn't actually *see* my mother meet Gary. I just know they did. And then one night she picked me up from Alexandra's house, after being out with him — with Gary.

"Isn't he cute?" my mother asked me. She was driving, and I was up front next to her. Anne was there, too, of course. She was sleeping in the backseat. Anne could sleep through anything.

It was dark, except for the dashboard lights and the beam of headlights on the narrow road that led to our house. I sat up front. I could see the strip of yellow rushing under the car, like it was being eaten up.

"No," I said.

"Oh, Leah. C'mon," my mother laughed. "He's *so* cute."

I yawned. Alexandra, Anne, Beth, and I had stayed up playing the Mystery Date electronic board game. We had already fallen asleep in the big bed. It was after midnight now.

"He's so special," she said. "So different."

I could tell by her tone of voice she was going to tell me something important, something grown-up and special. I tried to smother the end of my yawn in my sleeve.

"Sure," I said. I could feel her attention on me. I hoped Anne wouldn't wake up.

"Gary listens," my mother went on. "Your father never listened."

"I know." I heard myself saying. I regretted that instantly, but it didn't stop me from saying more. "He never listens to me either," I said.

There is something about being out this late at night that doesn't feel right. Being out after you've already gone to sleep isn't natural. People should be home in their beds. I could see — out my window — the stars outside, far away up in the black night.

"And Gary never — Oh, no!" my mother said suddenly.

I lifted my head. "What?" My heart started thumping immediately.

"I missed the turn. It's so damn dark," she said. She was looking behind her while driving forward. She was nervous.

"Are we lost?" I asked. I leaned toward the dashboard window, as if I could see something. I strained my eyes, as if I could figure it out if I looked hard enough. The darkness outside seemed suddenly oppressive, as if nothing could rise up and lift it away, as if it were going to be night forever.

My mother didn't answer me. She had her arm bent and up to her mouth, which is what she does when she is worried. She started clicking her teeth.

I looked out the window, but all I could see were trees, reaching with their black branches out at me. And the same yellow line in front of us, disappearing bit by bit as we moved forward.

"I don't know where we are," she said. "Damn!" She pulled the car over to the side of the road with a jerk, and then started to back up. I turned around to look.

"Watch out," I said.

"What!" she shouted back. "Don't just say *watch out.* What?"

"There's a ditch back there, Mom," I said.

"I know that!" she snapped.

She pulled the steering wheel over and over in the opposite direction and pulled forward again. She took a deep breath when we got back on the road.

"We're fine now," she said. "I know where we are."

As far as I could see the dark trees still reached out over the road in silhouettes.

We had to drive all the way back to Alexandra's road and start over before we could find our turn. My mother was laughing by the time we got to our house about one-thirty in the morning, but I wasn't.

She carried Anne inside, still sleeping.

Chapter Thirteen

*W*ill called me Sunday morning. It was the first phone call I had gotten since moving here with my dad and Gail. Gail came to my room to tell me.

"Leah? Phone," she said, knocking on my bedroom door.

I stepped out.

"For me?"

She nodded. She had her shoulders kind of hunched up, and she was smiling. "It's a boy," she whispered.

I could have allowed myself to step into the warmth of her voice, like a secret shared — but I didn't.

Instead I said, "It's just Will."

I walked into the kitchen to get the phone. It probably was "just Will," but for some reason, my heart rate was rapidly speeding up. Its beating was actually very annoying, like a mosquito or a turtleneck.

"Hello?" I said into the receiver.

"Hi, it's me."

It *was* Will.

I should have taken the portable phone, I thought. Although no one was around, I felt embarrassed. I pulled the cord as far as it would go, all the way toward the laundry room. I slipped inside and shut the door with the cord bent and wedged it flat.

"Leah? It's me, Will," he said again.

I crouched down by the washing machine.

"Oh, I know. Hi," I said into the phone.

"Oh, hey, do you have a bike?" Will asked me. "You want to go ride bikes?"

I had a bike in Phoenicia. I remember riding it, but it hadn't come to Shandaken with us, and I didn't have one here. But Gail did. I had seen it hanging in the garage. It was one of those bikes with the big tires and lots of gears, but it looked small enough. Gail wasn't much bigger than I was.

"Uh, I don't know," I said.

"What?"

"I mean, hold on. Okay?" But I didn't move. My knees were pressed up to my chest.

"I'll be right back, okay?" I said.

I stood up, but I didn't open the laundry room door.

I had never said Gail's name out loud. I had never even used it in a sentence, I don't think. I usually answered her in one-syllable sentences if at all possible. I had certainly never asked her for anything before.

"Are you still there?" Will said. "I mean, if you don't have one, that's okay. I didn't mean —"

"No, it's okay. Hold on, again," I said. I had to push hard to unstick the door where the cord was jammed. I lay the phone down on the kitchen counter.

"Gail?" I said out loud.

"In here," I heard her answer, and I headed into the living room. I heard her knitting needles clicking together.

Gail used to knit things (what a surprise) but only at night, after dinner, while my dad watched the news or read the paper. So she must have gone into the living room and started knitting in order to give me some privacy while I was on the phone. Gail finished counting something, and then looked up at me.

"Uh," I started, "can I . . . I mean, I think I saw . . . Do you have a bicycle in the garage?"

"Oh, sure," Gail said. She was standing up already.

"You want to use my bike?" She looked so eager I almost changed my mind. This was already against one of my rules, my rule that needing something means you owe someone. Owing someone something puts you at a disadvantage. And besides, it sets you up to be disappointed later when you need something again, but this time you don't get it. Better off not to have needed anything in the first place.

But I needed something. I really needed to borrow Gail's bike.

I nodded.

I *wanted* something. That's worse than needing it.

"Sure," Gail said. "Sure you can."

She was still smiling. I went back to the phone. Will and I made plans to meet by the old lumberyard, where Plains Road and the dirt road cross, by the river, near the Old Huguenot Cemetery, about two and a half miles from my house. My bus went that way every morning. It would be a flat ride the whole way.

"At noon," Will told me, and we hung up.

A few minutes later I was watching Gail show me how to switch gears and how to strap on the helmet. I thought, if she says "you're welcome," before I get a chance to say "thank you," I'll just explode.

But she didn't.

"Thanks," I said to Gail, as I rode down the driveway.

There was no turning back now.

Chapter Fourteen

*T*wenty minutes later I was at the lumberyard, sweat dripping down my back and itching me. I reached around and scratched my back. I pulled my shirt off my skin, lifting it up and down to let the air inside. It was quiet. Will wasn't here yet, so I looked around.

There was nothing about this rock, or this sky. Or this wind and this sun that was any different than it was a hundred years ago. Not even the old lumber building itself — if you could imagine it as it must have once been. Now it was really just a shell of a building, light filtering in through the many empty spaces in the walls. The floor only dirt. Tiny nails littered the ground.

The wind picked up in the air and blew the dried leaves into a loud chorus. It chilled my skin where it was wet. I was hot and cold at the same time.

I could be a boy, I thought.

Or I could be a slave girl who has run away, disguised as a boy and hiding in this abandoned lumberyard. At night I come out and sneak into the barns of the neighboring farmers looking for food. By day I sleep in the sawdust left on the dirt floor. I wear long trousers and suspenders. I cut my hair into a short, raggedy boy-style and bind my breasts with tightly wrapped cloth. (Well, so maybe I wouldn't need the binding.)

"Hello!"

Will's voice startled me. He had ridden his bike right up over the grass and up the sloping hill by the lumber building. He swung his leg over the center bar while the bike was still climbing upward. He jumped off. His bike rolled a few more feet and tipped over against a rock.

"Hey, I didn't hear you," I said. I felt warm again. I think my face was getting red, already. I hadn't even said anything stupid yet.

"Isn't this place awesome?" Will said.

"Yeah," I answered.

"I come here all the time," Will said.

He wandered over toward the edge of the slope, where the hill dipped toward the river. The grass was short; it was mostly moss. There were old trees, bent and skinny, and the leaves were vividly red and yellow and silvery green. Planks of wood that had fallen from the building lay gray and scattered and almost sunken into the ground. DUBOIS GRAIN AND LUMBER was barely visible in faded white paint, above where the door had once been but was now nothing more than an opening.

Everything here was a reminder that nothing was left, but something had once been.

Even Will looked like he could have lived here once, in this time. His vest, his baggy shirt, even the brown belt pulled too tightly and crunching up the waist of his jeans. His hair was straight and loose and gnarled in one spot in the back. He stood looking out toward the far mountains. He could have belonged to another time, except for his green sneakers. White socks, I noticed.

"You come here a lot?" I asked.

Will turned around.

"Yeah, because nobody else does," he said. "I like to run around."

The thought of that made me smile, and then it reminded of something from sleep-away camp. Sometimes the boys would come over from their side, at rest time, and chase the girls.

Funny, how it started. I don't know if we started running first or the boys started chasing us first. And I don't know that if we stopped running there would have been any chasing at all. But we did. We ran. It was exciting and scary. Some of the girls were laughing and giggling and not running very fast.

But I was.

I was really running. I was laughing, too, I guess. But I was nervous. I knew I didn't want to be caught. I was scared. I was running as fast as I could, and I am a *very* fast runner. When the boys caught the girls, they held them down, tickled them, or wrestled them. I never let myself be caught, and I learned that eventually boys will chase after the slower girls.

I don't know if I felt relieved or left out.

But with Will I wasn't scared, and I wasn't nervous.

"So you borrowed your mother's bike?" Will said. He sat down on one big boulder that seemed to grow out of the ground.

I sat beside him and folded my legs crisscross style. "Who?"

"Your mother. I heard you talking to someone. About the bike?"

"That was Gail," I said.

We both stared forward. The music of the leaves grew to a loud crescendo and then suddenly stopped. The sun, which had been behind a cloud, appeared like a spotlight switched on.

"Is Gail your stepmother?"

"No." I said it so fast. "She's not my stepmother." Too fast.

"Oh sorry," Will said. "I didn't mean . . . Well, hey, do you know who discovered lichen?"

"Discovered what?"

"Lichen. This green stuff on the rock." Will looked down and picked some off. He rolled it around in his fingers. His fingers were different than mine. He was so close. I could smell his body, cold air, laundry detergent, and warm skin.

"I thought it was just moss," I said.

"No, it's lichen. It's really two different plants living together. It's an alga and a fungus. They couldn't exist without each other. We learned about it in science. It's called communism or mutalism or something."

"Oh, yeah. I learned about that, too," I said.

Will held out his palm, and I took the soft plant into my hand.

"Together they look like one plant," Will said. "Isn't it beautiful?"

"It is beautiful," I said. "Or *they* are."

Will laughed. "And you know who discovered that lichen was really two plants?"

I shook my head.

"Beatrix Potter. You know, she wrote *Peter Rabbit* with Mr. MacGregor and all that?"

I nodded.

"Beatrix Potter was really a scientist first. She drew pictures of fungus and plants, but no one took her seriously. They told her to go home and draw more of those little pictures. So she did."

"Really?"

"Uh, huh."

"Did you learn that in science, too?" I asked.

"No. They don't teach you important stuff like that in school."

"Hmmm," I said.

If I moved an inch in either direction, if I lowered my back or my shoulders, I would have brushed against Will's shirt. My feet were getting pins and needles, but I didn't dare budge.

"Actually, my mother told me that stuff about Beatrix Potter," Will said. "She's like a feminist or something. But she works at IBM."

"Gail's not my stepmother," I said. " I mean, I don't call her that. I just hate that word. And not just because of the Cinderella story, either. It's like, *step*mother? What step is that exactly? Like, one more step and she's my *real* mother. Like you can measure your mother and see how much of a mother she is. A full step? Or half a step, and then she'd be real. Or would I? You know?"

Will was quiet. The absolute quiet of understanding.

"She seemed kind of nice on the phone," he said finally. "When I called, I mean. She seemed okay."

"She's not." I said. I was looking at the lichen in my hand. An alga *and* a fungus. How could anyone have ever seen that?

I put it down.

"Anyway, you can only have one real mother," I said. "So what's the point?"

Will was quiet again, but it was a different quiet, and then I remembered.

"Oh, I'm so sorry," I said right away. "I didn't mean for you. Being adopted or anything. I didn't mean about you."

The pins and needles in my foot had crept up my leg, and my whole left side was numb. But I didn't move. "I was just talking for myself. I mean, about me. I'm so sorry. Boy, I really talk too much."

"You can never talk too much. And I didn't think that, anyway," Will said, jumping up. "I was thinking about you. Not me. I never think of my mother as not my mother. Or my father."

I stretched out my legs and tried to stand.

"Sometimes I wonder about my birth mother," Will said. "I think someday I might want to find out — hey, are you okay?"

"Oh, I'm fine," I said, shaking my leg. I limped around holding on the side of the rock.

"Your foot fell asleep?" Will asked.

"Yeah. Bad."

Will laughed. "Well, there's nothing you can do about it. You've just got to run it off. Or better — ride it off. C'mon," he called.

And he took off down the hill toward our bikes. I didn't remember my homework promise to Mrs. Thomsen until I was on my way home, long after Will and I had ridden up the road by the river, and laughed, and felt the autumn wind in our faces.

But I decided that afternoon I would do my homework. For certain.

Chapter Fifteen

I wanted to show Will my poem. I didn't know why. It wasn't like I thought it was so good, but I liked it. And I liked doing it. And I didn't remember liking much, except riding bikes yesterday and sneaking to the auditorium every afternoon. And even lunchtime lately.

We had a routine. After lunch (Will and I ate lunch everyday by the shelves by the window) I went out the main doors where the cafeteria lady stood. I told her I had to go to the bathroom, which was out in the hall. Or sometimes I just nodded toward the girls' room, and she understood. She never seemed to notice that I never came back. I would stand inside the girls' room for a second or two (maybe just enough time to peek in the mirror and check my teeth) and then leave. I turned right out of the bathroom, not left, and I slipped away to the auditorium.

Will went outside, as if he were going for recess, and then he doubled back through the gym, which was always unlocked. He said he went right through the boys locker room and came out by the hall, near the music rooms and the auditorium.

"I wrote a poem for homework," I told Will.

We were sitting in the audience seats — dead center — eight rows back. Best seats in the house, Will said. The audience in a theater is called *the house*. I like that. The right side of the stage is called *stage left* and the left side is *stage right,* if you're looking at it from the audience's point of view.

Will was scrunched so far down in his chair that his legs were wrapped over the back of the seat in front of him.

"Let me hear it," Will said.

Even though that was exactly what I had wanted him to say, I suddenly became completely terrified.

"No, I can't," I said.

Will sat up. "Yeah, I want to hear it. Do you have it with you?"

I did. I had rewritten it two times and then typed it on my dad's computer. I printed it out twice. I had turned one copy into Mrs. Thomsen on Monday. The other copy had been folded in my pants pocket for two days now.

"No," I said. "It wasn't so good anyway. I just had to do it, you know. For homework."

"So let me just hear it. Don't you remember it? Some of it?"

I wanted to read my poem, but I just couldn't. I pulled the folded poem out of my pocket, and I held it.

"Oh, you have it. Can I see it?" Will asked, and I let the paper slip from my hand.

He opened it up and started reading out loud:

In the Hollow Empty Place

by Leah Baer

Left in the shadowy place that once was.
Empty windows and
         fallen lumber.
Gone are the busy sounds —
         of days gone by.
Of hopes and wishes
A hundred years past.
Upon this mossy rock —
Upon this hardened ground —
If you listen you can still hear the voices —
The crying.
The laughing
And the dreaming.

Let this splintered wood turn to horse-drawn carts
This hollowness to home.

Will held the paper in front of him for a few more long, long seconds. I could hardly take it. It had been hard enough to listen to my own poem. I could hardly wait for his reaction.

"It's beautiful," he said finally. Will looked over to me. "It's great. It's really great."

"Thanks," I said.

"I really mean it, Leah," Will said. "I think it's the best poem I've ever heard."

I knew if I brought my hand to my face it would be burning hot. It was the most wonderful, uncomfortable feeling I had ever had.

Chapter Sixteen

"Where were you at recess?" It was Sasha Buckley.

I looked up innocently from my desk. "What?" I asked, hoping for a few strategic moments to gather my thoughts and figure this one out.

"You weren't there," Sasha said.

"Well, I'm here now," I tried.

Sasha was leaning her whole body on the front of my desk. I knew Mr. Kelly was grading papers up at the front of the class, but of course I couldn't see him. The view was completely blocked.

Sasha ignored my brilliant attempt to throw her off.

"And neither was Will Hiller," Sasha went on. "And you're in school, and Will is in Megan O'Brien's class, and she says he's in school, too. So where were you?"

I tried to think of any movie I had seen where the hero

comes up with a great come-back line. Something so perfect and so truthful and just funny enough, with maybe a bad word or two. And then the bully (such as Sasha) knows instantly she is defeated by the sharp wit and quick tongue of the underdog (me, in this instance).

"Sasha, why don't you just mind your own beeswax?"

Did I really say that?

"What?" Even Sasha couldn't believe how stupid that was.

"I said, why don't you mind your own beeswax."

I said it again?

This time the kid next to me heard. It was Richard Malk, and he started laughing. Really loud.

Mr. Kelly looked up from his desk.

"Okay, okay. Enough. Miss Buckley you can sit down in your own seat," he said. "We are going to go over last night's homework. Everybody take out your books."

Sasha looked at me slowly, turned her eyes away, and then took her seat. Richard Malk was still laughing. Mr. Kelly started writing on the board. I took out my book and the notebook paper inside of it.

I *had* done my homework last night. In fact, I did all my homework the night before, too. And the night before that, I did *almost* all my homework.

"Let's put the answers up on the board today," Mr. Kelly said. "And show all work."

I did do my homework, but I certainly didn't know if

85

I had done it right or not. I sure wasn't about to raise my hand and volunteer to go up to the board. I slouched down against the back of my chair.

"Today, we're going to go right down the rows," Mr. Kelly said. "There were twenty-three problems. Twenty-three students —"

I slouched more.

There was still a chance, I thought. I was sitting in the back. Maybe he'll miss me. Mr. Kelly started by pointing to Liam Greenberg, who sat in front.

"Start with number one, Liam, and we'll go in order. When you're done, the next person can go, and so on. Leave enough room for five at the board at a time and begin the first problem about a foot from the top of the board. Three problems down in each column," he said. Then Mr. Kelly sat back at his desk and let the chaos begin.

The voices around me became a din through which I had to count with desperation.

If Liam had problem number one — I counted six people back — then the first person in the second row would get number seven. I counted the number of desks back. Someone was missing from the third row. That meant the fourth row began with problem eighteen. I could feel the wetness under my arms. My head started to hurt, but I was able to calculate that I would be given problem eighteen.

I threw open my book and double-checked number eighteen. Multiplying fractions. I hated multiplying fractions. Reducing. Yes, I had reduced. Cross multiply. I had cross-multiplied. I did it again just to make sure. One more time.

"Uh, Miss Baer?" Mr. Kelly's voice. "Do you have any idea what we are doing here?"

Apparently I didn't answer.

"Problem nineteen, Miss Baer," Mr. Kelly graciously explained. "And show your work."

Nineteen?

My eyes shot up to the front of the room. The girl who sat in front of me was at the board, and she was doing number eighteen. She was almost finished. The kid who hadn't been in his seat, three back, second row had come back from the bathroom.

I thought of a real good line to use on Sasha Buckley as I walked up to the board, a doozy. But I never could have said it out loud. Not in school, anyway. I began copying my work onto the board. Problem nineteen.

If Sasha found out where Will and I were going during recess, everything would be ruined. Funny thing was, after all that — I would have gotten problem number eighteen wrong.

Nineteen, I had right.

Chapter Seventeen

*W*ill came to school late the next day. I remembered he said he had an orthodontist appointment. We were going to meet in the auditorium.

He wasn't at lunch, and I didn't have time to warn him. He was already there, up on the stage pacing back and forth. He spun around when he heard me slip in through the big auditorium doors. He had this big smile on his face.

He won't be smiling for long, I thought.

He wouldn't be smiling after I told him that Sasha Buckley knew we had both been skipping recess, when I told him that we were probably going to get caught and get in big trouble. Detention or worse. Worse — we wouldn't be able to come here anymore.

I didn't think I could bear that.

The auditorium was so familiar by now. The carpet down the center was worn where the years of audiences walked, took their programs, and sat in their seats. There were sticky spots on the stage from all the different marks of masking tape showing the actors where to stand. There were the seats that creaked when they were folded down and ones that wouldn't go back up without a big push.

"Will, I have to tell you something," I began. I started down the aisle.

"I have to tell you something first," Will said.

"No, I have to tell you something . . ."

Will jumped up onto the stage. He was waving a paper in the air. "Okay, what?" Will said. "But hurry. I have to tell you something."

And then I couldn't do it. He looked so happy about whatever it was.

"Okay, okay. You go first," I said.

"Look!" he said. "An audition. They are holding auditions for the play. I've seen it every year. And this year, I thought, maybe this year . . . we could be in it. You and me."

"An audition?" I said.

"Yeah, a tryout," Will said . "For the middle-school play."

"For what?"

Will took a deep breath and tried to slow down.

"They do a production here every year. This year it's a

play by Kurt Vonnegut, Jr. That's what it says here," Will said. He held out the flyer to me. "Mr. Calabrini is going to be the director."

I realized Will was serious.

How many times I had imagined loud voices quieting to a hush as the lights dimmed. I imagined standing on stage singing or dancing the way I did with Will. But no more than I imagined being a pioneer or a kind Indian woman's daughter.

"I can't be in a play," I said.

"Why not?" Will asked.

Why not?

Because there was something permanent about being in a play. There would be rehearsals and a schedule and then a play, a performance, a commitment. I never really thought about being here that long. Not really. It was sort of day by day. Homework by homework. Test by test. Letter by letter.

I couldn't try out for a play, could I?

And suddenly, I realized I hadn't written to my mother in a long while, not since I had written that poem or took that math test — not in days. Maybe weeks. I hadn't told her about bike riding. About the lumberyard. Or the color of the leaves. A whole season had gone by. It was almost winter.

And then I got scared. Was I forgetting already? So quickly. I felt like I was falling.

"No, I definitely can't," I told Will. I handed the flyer back to Will.

"Yeah, maybe you're right," Will said, looking at the paper in his hand. "I can't do it either. What was I thinking? It's mostly seventh and eighth graders. Mostly eighth graders really. Even if they suck. They'd give a part to an eighth grader before a sixth grader."

We both sat down on the edge of the stage, looking out. I didn't know what to say. Maybe there was a time I would have agreed. I would have wanted something like this, too.

But I was afraid.

"Can I tell you something?" Will began.

"Sure," I said.

"I mean, you can't tell anyone. Okay?"

I couldn't imagine what Will would tell me that he wouldn't want anyone else to know, but I knew if he wanted to tell me, I would listen.

"Promise."

"I want to be famous," Will said softly.

"You do?"

Will let his feet bang against the wooden stage. He was always moving, some part of him was always in motion. The whole theater was before us, seats folded up as if they were listening, too.

"I can't explain it better than that," Will said. "It's not like I want lots of money or to have people recognize me when I walk down the street. I just want to be something . . . different. Something special. Sometimes, I want it so bad it hurts."

Will already *was* something special. But I understood, and I didn't say anything. Sometimes I wanted something so bad it hurt, too.

"I just have to do *something*. I have to," Will said. "I mean, I can feel it . . . even though, it's inside me, I can almost touch it."

"But what if you never get what you want," I whispered.

"Well," said Will very slowly. "I've thought about that and —"

"And?"

"And I think the worse thing would be to live your whole life without a dream."

"Even if it never comes true?"

"Yes," Will said.

I wondered if he was right about that. And I wondered if you had to let go before you could hold onto anything. But I wasn't sure.

"Do you think dreams can come true?" I asked.

Will looked right at me. "Yes," he said. "I'm sure of it."

Will smiled. He put his hand down, and I put mine down right next to his. We weren't touching, but we were close enough to imagine it, to dream.

Chapter Eighteen

Actually, it was Gary.

Gary was really into hippie stuff and mysticism and things like that. He didn't know it (and I would never have told him), but it was Gary who taught me how to dream.

Gary burned incense and read tarot cards and had big posters of Hare Krishna on the walls of his room in Alexandra's mother's house. He had long beads hanging down instead of a door. He talked a lot about Eastern religions and holy men. I used to hear him telling my mother stories, as if they were real. Or real things that sounded like stories.

They were kind of interesting though. And when he was around, I listened. I pretended I wasn't. But I listened.

Of course, my mother got really into it. And that year for Halloween, in fifth grade, she made me a costume instead of buying one. It was an Indian sari. It was a long layer of beautiful material all wrapped around me, down to my feet and over my head, even across my mouth. My mother painted my eyes with black eyeliner and put a dot in the middle of my forehead. I wanted to love it because she did. So I said I did.

But during the school parade kids made fun of me, and I couldn't walk very well. I decided not to go trick-or-treating. I just took Anne around town in Shandaken.

She shared all her candy with me anyway. I knew she would.

Gary talked a lot about Hindu priests who could control their minds. He said it took a very strong mind and years of practice, but some of them had learned to actually stop their heartbeats or leave their physical bodies and fly over the entire earth, through time and space. Some of these men spent years with one arm raised in the air or standing on one leg to prove their power. It was all about control. Mind control.

Even though I knew I would probably never be able to leave my body and fly over the world (though that would have been nice), I was fascinated. And I thought I could learn to control my mind, even just a little.

It seemed like a very useful thing to be able to do.

The first thing I learned to do was turn myself into a piece of furniture.

This was more a practical way of sitting through dinner when Gary was over; I hated it when Gary was over. I found it came in pretty handy at school, too. Like when the teacher was yelling at the class or when I got in trouble. Usually for talking too much. Or talking while the teacher was talking. Or saying something I shouldn't have been saying whether the teacher was talking or not.

I would hear the words coming out of the teacher's mouth, but my body would melt into the wood I was sitting on. I would become hard and unmoving like the chair. I'd get detention, but I wouldn't cry. Chairs don't cry.

But the second thing I taught my brain to do was just for fun.

I learned to control my dreams.

It took a lot more practice, but it was worth it. After a few weeks of concentrating and willing my mind to focus, I found I could actually *give* myself a dream.

I had to do it at night, of course, in bed just before I would start to fall asleep. The trick was to stay awake but just allow yourself to slip into that in-between time, when all things become real. I had to work very hard to escape from my actual body, which was lying in my bed, and get smaller and smaller until I was entirely inside my brain. Then I could dream whatever I wanted. And it felt real.

I could dream that I was a princess and had been living this peasant life as a test of my strength and bravery. The truth would emerge, and I would be taken off to my castle and all my fancy clothes. Everyone there would be amazed by my humbleness and my beauty. (It *was* a dream, after all.)

I could dream I was discovered to be the fastest girl runner in the school, and I am sent to the Olympics, where I win a gold medal. My heart would nearly burst when they played the national anthem.

Or I could dream that there is a big, disastrous fire in the school, and everyone panics, including the teacher, and only I have the presence of mind to put blankets over the flames and lead everyone out to safety. Then all the kids are so grateful. One of the boys, who laughed at me for wearing a sari on Halloween, invites me over to his house for a sandwich and swim in his pool.

But I say no.

Chapter Nineteen

"I suppose you think I don't know where you two are going at recess everyday," Sasha said, stopping me in the hall outside of Mr. Kelly's room.

Will had left the auditorium first. Then I had counted to "thirty-Mississippi" and followed. I was heading toward math class. I was thinking about the play, about auditions and costumes and scripts. And I never got to tell Will about what Sasha had said. In fact, I had forgotten all about Sasha.

Until just now.

"I don't know what you're talking about," I said, as if that would work.

It didn't.

"And, like, we're supposed to think something's going on in there?"

"In where?" I said, straining to think. Why can't I come up with a good line when it could actually do some good?

"But Will Hiller's so gay. Probably nothing is even happening," Sasha said. She blocked my way and she was staring right at me, like she was searching for something.

Then she laughed, apparently with satisfaction, "You don't even have a hickey." She snorted, actually.

For someone who had spent a month at sleep-away camp, I probably should have known what a hickey was. In fact, somewhere in the back of my mind I thought I had heard about hickeys. I thought it had something to do with boy and girl stuff, with chasing and being caught, and red spots on people's necks. And somehow at that moment, I knew I needed to do something.

"Oh, yes I do. I have a huge hickey," I told Sasha.

I wasn't covering up for Will, because he didn't need that, and he never would. And I wasn't doing it for myself, because right then and there I decided I *would* try out for the play. With Will. And I couldn't wait to tell him, so he could sign us up before the end of the day.

I was doing it for Sasha. Because there are some people in this world that won't shut up any other way.

I pulled up my collar and smiled. "You just can't see it."

Sasha stared at me harder.

"You do not," she said, narrowing her eyes.

"How do you know?" I said.

It wasn't my worst line, but it wasn't awful. And it must have worked to some degree.

Sasha was speechless.

I walked right past her and into the classroom.

Chapter Twenty

"I have something to show you," my dad was saying.

I had just walked into the house. I had been imagining being in the middle-school play the whole ride home on the bus. Even though it *couldn't* happen. Could it? Wouldn't happen. No. But I gave myself a daydream, and it made the ride go faster.

"Leah?" My dad said. "Did you hear me? Come and see."

My dad waved me toward my room, and I followed.

My room was pale yellow when I picked it, and Gail made me sheer yellow curtains that matched the brightness of the walls. I thought the curtains were frilly and girly, and I never said thank you (or maybe I mumbled it), but every time I walked into my room I was greeted by my curtains. And I loved them.

When my windows were open, the curtains blew out with the wind like they were alive and dancing. When there was a storm coming, the wind sucked them up against the screen like they were trying to escape. Now that it was cold out and the windows were closed, they hung patiently.

And I had begun collecting again. Already the top of my bureau was full. I had two pictures that Will had made, propped up against the back wall. One was a bird, and it looked so real I thought it was watching me. Every feather was drawn. Even the branch and the bird's claw wrapped around it looked perfect. The other picture was a nest, delicate and tiny, and inside were two round eggs with names painted on the sides. *Leah.* And *Will.*

I also had a cardboard box filled with tiny things, coins, special pretty rocks, a piece of smooth rounded glass I had found walking to the bus. I had a new jewelry box that Gail had given me. I had seen the box in her room, and Gail said she didn't want it anymore when I said I thought it was pretty. It was covered with blue material and tiny mirrors all around it and little beads in between the little mirrors.

I had a lot of stuff. And now, apparently, I had a new bed.

"Do you like it?" my dad was asking me.

It was beautiful. It was iron, but it was painted white.

The headboard had swirly circles that came together into one big circle with a flower, clover thingy in the center. It had four posts, and on top of each post was a round knob the color of copper. It was beautiful.

"I saw it on my way home. At a yard sale. But it's in good shape," my dad said. "I just finished putting it together."

He had worked hard. That bed must be heavy. I noticed my dad looked kind of tired.

"Just be careful. Don't jump on it or anything. It doesn't have a bedspring, just those boards underneath. So be careful," my dad said.

"I will."

"Do you like it?" he asked again.

I loved it. I almost told him then, about the play, about the auditions, about Will, maybe even let him hear my poem. But I stopped myself. I wasn't sure.

"It's nice, Dad," I said, and I walked over and reached my arms over his shoulders. I was tall, taller than last time I had done this. But not too tall.

"I love it."

I hugged my dad, and when he hugged me back I got scared all over again. I didn't know if I was ready to be here. All the way. Completely.

It was almost as if I was scared of not being scared. Either way, I still wasn't sure.

Dear Mom,

I am so sorry that I haven't written in so long.
I will write a really long letter to make up for it.

Mostly what's going on are these auditions for
the middle-school play. Will called me and told me
when my audition time was. There were only a few
choices left by the time he signed us up. I thought
we'd get to go together, but I guess not. I hope
I can find the right room. It's in the eighth-grade
hall. I've never been down the eighth-grade hall.

The play is really from a book called Welcome to
the Monkey House. It's by Kurt Vonnegut Jr. Have
you ever heard of him? I sort of did. So, I just
looked him up on the internet and he looks like an
author you would really like. I also found out that
Kurt Vonnegut is an artist, too. He paints and
draws and makes sculptures. I read that a lot
of his books, like Welcome to the Monkey House, have
been banned.

I can't wait to read it.

The director is a teacher in the school and it
sounds like you would really like him, too. I heard
that he's really cool. I've seen him in the halls. Will
pointed him out to me. His name is Mr. Calabrini
and he teaches 7th and 8th grade English. He
wears big huge glasses, and he has a beard that
looks like it's all part of the same big hair on his

head. He's really skinny and I think he smokes cigarettes because when you pass him in the hall he smells like a smokestack. But everybody loves him. The older kids hang out in his room and talk about books. I heard he doesn't believe in grades and he gives everybody an A.

Hope I get him next year. It would be nice to see something like that on my report card. Even a B would be nice.

And the last thing I'm going to tell you is about this girl in my class who hates me. Her name is Sasha. Today in math, she started the I-Hate-Leah-Baer Club. She had a sign-up sheet stuck under her math book and hanging off the end of her desk. Whenever Mr. Kelly walked by she just pulled it up under her book. I tried to act like I didn't even notice it, which seemed to work pretty well. Actually, I don't think anyone really noticed it. Except me.

She may be planning on blackmailing me because she knows that I don't go out for recess. But so far, nothing.

Well, gotta go. Miss you so much.

Love, Leah

PS: By the way, is a hickey a bad thing or a good thing? Or just a stupid thing. That's what I thought.

Chapter Twenty-one

 I found the eighth-grade hall. And the right room. The boy who had the audition time before me was finished. He opened the door and stepped out. I didn't know who he was, but we nodded to each other.

Now it was my turn.

I looked back to the boy who had just came out. I was going to say something like, How'd you do? But he was already halfway down the hall. He must have been running.

Inside the music room, I could see Mr. Calabrini sitting in a chair. He was wearing all black, shirt and jeans. Even his shoes. He had his legs crossed tightly and crossed again at his ankles. He motioned for me to come in.

Mr. Calabrini was holding a clipboard.

"Hello? Um, Leah. Leah Bear?" Mr. Calabrini asked me. "B-E-A-R?"

"Yeah, um, no. It's Baer. B-A-E-R," I said. Will must have spelled my name wrong.

Mr. Calabrini's glasses took up most of his face. But I could see his eyes, looking right at my eyes. That always makes me uncomfortable. But this time I remembered something that Gail had told me, about how it's polite to look someone in the eye when they are speaking to you. Normally, I wouldn't *think* of doing something Gail was trying to make me do. I wouldn't *consider* it. But something told me I should look Mr. Calabrini in the eye. Maybe even smile.

I looked at Mr. Calabrini and smiled. Mr. Calabrini smiled back.

"Well then, Leah Baer, let's get started."

I took a deep breath, and when I let it out it sounded like a wobble, like when you blow air straight into a running fan. Will and I had practiced and practiced, but I never planned for how nervous I was going to be.

I was extremely nervous.

"Are you ready?" Mr. Calabrini asked me.

No, I thought.

Yes, I nodded.

"I'd like to see you do some improvisation," Mr. Calabrini said. "Do you know what that means?"

Did I?

"Like pretending something. Acting it out?" I tried.

"Well, yes. It means acting without a script. So you

can do anything you'd like and not have to be prepared," he said.

Well, I should be great at this, I thought, because I definitely wasn't prepared. I had imagined that I would be reading something. Acting, like Will and I did in the auditorium.

"So first, I want you to show me getting up in the morning."

"What?" I managed to say. "What do you want me to do?"

"Just go with it. Be loose," Mr. Calabrini said, leaning back in his chair. He uncrossed his legs and recrossed them the other way, even tighter.

"Give it all you've got," he said.

Panic is a very amazing thing. It comes over you almost like, I imagine, a flesh-eating virus would do. It just takes over. The first thing to go is your brain and your ability to think. But quickly you realize it has also taken over your ability to move. Or speak clearly.

"Getting up in the morning?" I squeaked out.

Mr. Calabrini nodded and appeared to be writing something on his clipboard already. There was no time to panic. My whole life and all my dreams were slipping away, being *yanked* away, and I was doing nothing to stop it.

I took another breath.

Getting up in the morning? Well, that's easy. After all, I do get up every morning.

So should I start out asleep with my eyes closed? Should I actually lay down on the floor or just pretend to be laying down? If I lay down and pretend I'm sleeping, would that really be acting? Or just napping?

So far I was just standing in the middle of the room with my eyes closed. And it probably didn't look very exciting or particularly talented.

I opened my eyes.

Should I stretch my arms, like in the cartoons? And then yawn or something?

Should I —

"Thank you. That was terrific," Mr. Calabrini was saying.

But I hadn't done anything.

If somehow I were invisible and watching this whole scene it might actually make me laugh. It was ridiculous. It was hilarious. But I certainly wasn't laughing. I was feeling sick.

In fact, I must have looked like I was about to throw up.

"Leah, are you feeling all right? Leah?" Mr. Calabrini asked me.

And right then and there I knew it was all over.

Chapter Twenty-two

As soon as I got off the bus, I ran inside my house. I didn't stop in the kitchen. I didn't take off my coat. I didn't stop and see what was on TV.

I didn't stop. If I stopped I would have to think.

I snuck past Gail, who was in the kitchen.

So how was school today?, she would have asked. Like she always does.

How was school? It sucked. Oh, what was that? Oh, right. It sucked, no, thank you.

I ran to my room. I took my binder out of my backpack. And my books, my lunch card, and everything that drops to the bottom. I dumped it all onto my bed. All of it, all my stuff, all the stuff that had collected in my backpack since I started school here. I didn't even look at it, only to see the crumbs stuck to old papers, and wrappers from candy I didn't remember having. Imagine that in only a few months a whole lifetime of stuff can accumulate, enough to have been forgotten already. Enough to be garbage.

I left it all where it was and went into the kitchen.

There was a brand new box of granola bars in the pantry. I grabbed it, the whole box, and dropped it into my backpack. I also took a bag of chips with a rubber band around it. A full bottle of Juicy Juice. There were three Milano cookies left in the bag. A box of Pop-Tarts, strawberry. With frosting. A jar of unsalted peanuts — half full. Mini-marshmallows. I generally don't like marshmallows, but I took them.

I took it all.

"What are you doing?" It was Gail.

"Nothing," I said. Nothing is the standard answer. It works about eighty-five percent of the time. Not this time.

"What are doing?" she asked again.

"I'm leaving," I said, and that's when I knew what I was doing.

My backpack was so heavy I had to set it on the ground in order to zip it up. The bottle of juice clanked against the jar of peanuts. When I lifted it up and swung it over my shoulders it sagged and pulled. And clanked.

"No, you're not," Gail said, as strongly, I suppose, as she could manage.

I didn't even answer her. It was as if she weren't there, which was how it had been all along really. And I guess she knew it, too.

I hurried out to the garage, to Gail's bike leaning against the wall. I pulled up the garage door and wheeled the bike outside. It was cold. It was freezing. The little tiny hairs inside my nose tightened up instantly, and it made me sneeze.

I was leaving.

I pushed off with one foot and swung my other leg over the back of the bike. The weight of all that food made me wobble. It shifted from one side to the other, and I almost fell. But as soon as I started peddling I was balanced again. And once I had started moving, I kept going.

My knuckles felt raw and dry. I wished I had thought to bring gloves. Instead of this bottle of juice. My back hurt. My cheeks, which had been stinging, were now numb, but I kept riding. I kept blinking to shut out the cold wind.

It seemed only my legs knew where I was going. Until I saw the tip of the old wooden building come into view, I didn't know where that was. I was almost warm by the time I got there. Well, I was cold but sweating. I couldn't feel my toes. Or my fingers. Or the tip of my nose.

I left the bike by the hill, and I followed my feet to the big rock by the edge of the grass. Everything was cold and hard. Even the lichen was stiff. It flicked off in little pieces. The leaves on the trees around me were no longer red and gold, but mostly brown and curled like dry paper. They covered the ground in a brittle blanket. Two squirrels chasing each other sounded like an army of crunching feet.

I wanted to cry but nothing came out. I broke out the granola bars. I ate two, no problem.

᚛᚛

I can't eat a granola bar without thinking of my mother. My mother went through this kick right after we moved out from Dad's. She stopped eating meat and she made things that had seaweed as an ingredient. She never took the TV out of the box after we moved to Shandaken, and she stopped buying the kind of cereal I liked. She stopped buying cookies and pretzels. But for some reason she let me eat granola bars.

I knew that granola bars tasted too good to *really* be health food, but I wasn't about to say anything. It was the closest thing to candy I got to have. It got worse when she met Gary, and he grew his own vegetables in his garden. The only thing that seemed to grow was zucchini and a few tomatoes. But lots of zucchini.

I hate zucchini more than anything in this world. I hated the smell of it and especially the slimy feel of it. I hated the taste of it. I can't even spell it.

One of those nights I can hardly remember, but I'll never forget. Just before I left for camp, we were eating dinner. Gary had just started to live with us. He used to cook dinner some nights. Of course, he made zucchini.

Naturally, I refused to eat it.

Gary got really mad. I remember Anne started quietly crying. I remember my mother didn't say anything. She was silent.

But not me. I had something to say, and if I couldn't say it with words, I'd say it anyway. Gary wanted me to eat the zucchini.

It was him against me — all the way. Everyone else had finished eating and had had ice cream, vanilla; and then everything was cleared away, except for me and my plate of zucchini. But I still didn't eat it.

I suppose I tried a little. I took big gulps of milk so I wouldn't taste it or feel it. But when my milk was gone and the zucchini wasn't, I stopped trying.

It was eight-thirty at night when Gary finally gave up. He didn't like me to begin with, and he *really* didn't like me after that.

❧

I WAS THIRSTY, now, but my hands were too cold to take out the juice. I wanted to cry so badly, but I wouldn't.

Chapter Twenty-three

*T*here was nothing about this rock, or this sky; or this wind and this sun that was any different than it was a hundred years ago. Or two hundred. I could be anybody. I could have been a runaway slave. I came over on a boat from England. My parents were criminals. Not really bad criminals, it's just that they were so poor. They sold me to pay their debts, and I had to go live with a Puritan family in Connecticut, sort of like Kit in *The Witch of Blackbird Pond*. Except that she had been wealthy, I think. Anyway, I had to sweep the sawdust from the floor of Dubois Grain and Lumber. And the animal droppings. And I had to fetch drinking water from the river. (It was very clean in those days.)

They worked me so hard, till my fingers and my feet were bleeding. In the winter they didn't give me shoes. I got frostbite, and they had to cut off three of my toes on my left foot and one on my right. Everything was bleak and sad and miserable, but I could still dream, laying on my bed of straw.

And dreams could still come true, couldn't they?

"Leah? Are you here?" It was Will's voice from the other side of the building. "I see your bike. I know you're here."

"Will?" I shouted.

His face was all red, and he was breathing hard. His breath was a cloud that blew out in white bursts.

"How did you know I was here?" I asked. "How did you get here?"

"I just thought you'd be here. When your step-mother . . . your mother . . . I mean, when your Gail said you left. And she sounded really upset. And when she said you left on your bike, I knew. I mean, I guessed," Will said. "So it was *that* bad? The audition?"

"Worse," I said.

Will was quiet.

"You called? You talked to Gail?" I asked. "Did you tell her where I was?"

"No, I didn't really figure it out until after I hung up."

The sun was already red and dipping below the old lumber building. The coldness crept up through my clothes. This must truly be what it feels like to freeze to death. Actually, I read that freezing to death is a warm sensation that overcomes you just before you slip away. It's supposed to be very peaceful and calm. I guess I was not dying.

"Then I won't do it, either," Will said.

"Do what?"

"I won't be in the play either. I mean, that is, if I get a part I won't take it."

"What?" I said.

Will came and sat beside me. I could feel his warmth instantly.

"I won't do it either," Will said. "It's just a play."

I thought about what he was saying, what he was offering. His dream. As if giving up his dream would help me find mine. I felt like crying again but not about the play or the audition. Or about the cold or the bad stomachache I was now having. It was something entirely different. Like living a life and never knowing what your dream is because you are too afraid. Or too angry.

"No, that isn't it," I said.

"What is it then?"

"My mother's not coming back for me," I told Will.

He didn't say anything.

"I think I kind of told you that she was. And that I would be going to California with her, but I'm not. I never was. I haven't even heard from her in months. Three. Three months. But it doesn't matter how long it was. I knew it right away."

It was really freezing out. My body started to tremble with a shiver that started way inside and worked its way out.

"You're cold," Will said. "We should go."

"No, I'm okay. I want to tell this." I said. "Because that's *still* not all of it."

And I let go. I stopped lying.

"My mother's not really my mother. I mean, not my *real* mother," I said.

I explained. "Right after my mother died — and I don't remember her at all — my father married Karen, that's her name, Karen. And I started calling her *Mom,* I guess because I was so little. So she was just always my mom. After a few years, my little sister was born, and it was like there just was no difference. I never even thought about it. About my real mom or any mom but her. I guess like you and your mom."

Will nodded.

"So when my dad and mom, well, my dad and Karen — It sounds so weird. Karen. Well, when they got divorced, I stayed with her, not my dad. I just lived with my sister and my mom."

I heard my voice in the air pick up and blow away with my words, with the leaves. I knew what I was saying, but I didn't still feel anything when I said it. I didn't even feel like crying anymore.

"I haven't seen my sister in three months, either. My

dad says she's going to visit us soon. I mean, he tried to talk to me about it, but I don't want to hear it. He says he's got a lawyer and everything. So that's it. My mom isn't my mom, not really. And she's not coming back. There I said it."

"No wonder you're so angry," Will said.

"What do you mean? I'm not angry."

"Well, that was a real messed-up thing for her to do." Will sounded angry. "It was a horrible thing for a mother or anyone to do."

"That doesn't make me feel much better," I said.

"It's not supposed to," Will said. "Look, maybe there's a right place for everyone. And some people are born in that place, and some people aren't."

"So was that supposed to make me feel better?"

Will nodded. "Yeah, so maybe you have to find that place. And if you're lucky, you find it sooner rather than later. But you find it," Will said. "Or it finds you."

"Like I found *you,*" I said.

Will smiled. "No, like *I* found you. Remember?"

For some reason, it seemed a good moment to eat a Pop-Tart. I opened up my backpack.

"Jeez, how long were you going away for?" Will asked looking inside.

"I wasn't going anywhere," I said. "I don't *have* any-where to go." Slowly the anger inside began to leak out. And the pain. And the sadness. All at once.

"You don't have to go anywhere," Will said. "Because you already *are* somewhere."

"Where's that?" My words barely slipped out in front of my tears.

"Here," Will said. He looked over at me. "Oh, no, don't cry."

"I'm not crying," I said.

Will jumped up. He nearly tripped over all the food.

"So tell me about something else, then," he said. "But don't cry. I didn't mean to make you cry. So what about your sister? I didn't even know you had a sister. What's her name?" Will was trying so hard. He was definitely trying.

"Anne," I said. "My sister's name is Anne."

And I started to cry.

Chapter Twenty-four

Anne and I never, ever, used the word *half-sister*.

I remember being in town, in Woodstock once with Anne and Mom. Somebody, some older lady, was talking to us. We were in line at the supermarket. The old lady was behind us, talking and talking.

Anne and I weren't really listening. We were counting the candy in the display. Mom had to run back to get something she forgot from the shelf. The old woman was left staring at us. She seemed more uncomfortable with that than we were.

"Are you two friends?" She asked.

I blurted it out. "We're sisters," I said.

"Oh, but you two look nothing alike."

And that was true. Anne and I look nothing alike, and we knew it. Anne was light. I was dark. Anne had thin straight hair, like her mother. I had dark, wavy hair. Anne was tiny. She had freckles. She had blue eyes.

I was not tiny. I had one beauty mark (my dad called it that) right by the side of my lips. I had dark brown eyes and no freckles.

"I'd never have guessed you two were sisters." The woman was still talking. "Not in a million years."

Anne and I started smiling at each other.

We would never explain. There was nothing to say. We were sisters.

Anne was the quiet one. I was loud. I talked too much. Anne liked to keep the peace. I wanted to fight for it. It got me into a lot of trouble.

"So who cares?" I said to the woman.

"Oh, my," she said. I think she took her five cans of tomato soup, her loaf of bread, her cat food, and went into the next line.

"Who cares what you think?" I shouted after the old lady.

But when my mother decided to leave for good, she took Anne, and she didn't take me.

Chapter Twenty-five

My father was standing in his underwear in the kitchen. I could see him through the window as I peddled down the driveway. The light was on above the sink.

My tears had long since evaporated or were frozen to my eyelashes. I had cried so long, I started laughing. Then I told him about my audition, and Will started laughing, too. I made it real funny. But it was getting dark, and Will had a much longer ride home. All uphill.

We rode off in opposite directions, and I promised Will I would call his mom and let her know he was on his way home, since I would be back long before he would.

Well, my dad wasn't totally in his underwear exactly. It looked more like he had come home from work and started to undress and change, but stopped somewhere in the middle. Somewhere in the middle of his dress pants and his jeans. He still had his shirt on but no tie. He had his dress socks on but no shoes.

He had his hand on the counter by the sink, and the other hand up to his head, rubbing his temples up and down. Up and down. That was his angry motion.

It was dark and late, and I had never told anyone where I was going. All that food I took. My dad must be really, really mad at me.

I decided it would not be a good idea to come into the house this way. I left Gail's bike outside the garage and ducked around the side of the house. I could use the front door, which nobody uses, and sneak into my room. I could slip right into my room.

I could see the hall clock as I walked by. It was 6:38. I remembered my promise to Will. I had to call his parents and let them know he was on his way.

Very quietly I turned the handle on the front door. It was usually unlocked. Nobody from the street wandered out this way. Nobody could even tell our driveway was a driveway. My dad only locked the door at night, and sometimes even then he forgot.

Click.

It was open.

Maybe I could have gotten away with it. I could have just come out of my room very nonchalant, and when my father stood there in his underwear I would announce that I had been in my room the whole time.

123

"I don't know what everyone is so upset about. I know it's late. I just need to make a quick phone call.

Oh, well I was in my room doing my homework and oh, I must have been concentrating so hard I didn't hear. Oh, I must have just been in the bathroom when —"

It was a plan.

But when I slipped into my room, Gail was sitting on my bed, a pile of scattered paper next to her. She was concentrating so deeply that she didn't hear me walk in. I stood watching her for a moment. It took me a whole, long second to realize what she was doing. My letters.

She was looking at my letters.

My bureau drawer was open. My letters were on the bed. Letters to my mother.

Each letter was in a envelope. Each was stamped.

And each envelope was addressed simply: TO MOM.

To Mom.

Because I didn't know what to write. I didn't know the street or town or city. I didn't know her address.

Gail whisked around.

"Oh, Leah," she said jumping up. "It's dark out. It's so late. Where were you?"

She must have momentarily forgotten that she was snooping through my stuff. She had gone into my room, into my drawer. Way in the back of my drawer, under my underwear. I had kept her out of my life, out of my conversations, my school, my whole life — and here she was.

I didn't say anything. I didn't move. I braced myself from the inside. She saw me staring at the bed, at my letters. At my stuff.

"Well, we were worried," Gail said. "You just took off. Do you know what time it is?"

"So what were you're doing in here?" I shouted. "Checking the time?"

Gail stood up. "Young lady, you are way out of line. You're the one who should be explaining. I was looking for where you might have gone. A name. A friend's. Anything. I was looking for you," she said. Her voice was trembling.

"In my underwear drawer?"

"Yes!" she shouted back.

"I hate you!" I screamed. It came out. It came out from a place so deep inside me. It was a powerful word, and I knew it.

I was afraid. So afraid. And I was angry. Really angry.

"I hate you. I hate you!" I said again. And again.

I saw Gail's eyes fill up with tears, and I was glad. I was winning.

"I was just trying —" Gail shouted back. "You never let me help. . . . You're always so awful to me!"

I was definitely winning. But what I didn't know.

"Just get out!" It was my voice.

I heard my father's footsteps. Then he was standing in the doorway.

"What's going on?" he said. He was looking around the room, as if there was some answer there.

"I hate you, too," I said. I said it loud. It actually felt good to shout. I wanted to shout more. I wanted to scream.

"I hate both of you," I screamed.

"It doesn't matter," Gail said. "She's back." She was crying and gathering up the letters. Then she stopped. She didn't touch them again. She left them on the bed.

My dad looked at Gail. I knew the look, and I knew the silence. He wasn't going to say what he really thought. He was going to be the grown-up and side with the other grown-up. He would save the psychobabble for later.

"That doesn't explain why it's almost seven o'clock and you've been out, and it's dark and you didn't tell anyone where you were," my dad spoke. His rational psychologist voice.

"Jeff, stop. She's home now. It's not the time for this," Gail was saying.

"We will talk about this later," my dad said finally. It was over for now. Then I remembered.

"No, wait. I have to call Will's parents," I spoke up. "I have to tell them he's on his way home."

"We've already spoken to them. Three times," my dad

said. "I'll call the Hillers and tell them you're back." He motioned that he was going to leave. He held the door for Gail to do the same.

Gail looked back at the bed. "I didn't look at them," she said. "I mean, I didn't open them. I didn't read them. I just thought — we were worried about you. I didn't read them. I promise."

My father shut my door behind them. I listened as their footsteps moved away down the hall. I heard the door open in the kitchen. I waited another five minutes or so before I could move. I was so tight, my legs, my back, even my head ached.

Finally I looked over to my bed. At my letters.

To Mom. That's all. No address. No return address. They would never have gotten anywhere.

Chapter Twenty-six

I could hear my Dad and Gail fighting, or as they call it, "discussing things," in their room. I was already in bed but I couldn't fall asleep, and I had no dreams to give myself that night. That time and space between falling asleep and being awake was empty.

I got out of bed and stepped quietly across the floor. I opened the door very slowly at first and then very quickly, right at the point when I knew it would creak. I took two steps out into the hall to hear better. I stood perfectly still, and if ears can be stretched, I stretched my ears. I listened as hard as I could.

"You've got to talk to her, Jeff. She's your daughter. She's not your patient, for God's sake," Gail's voice, obviously.

"I've tried. Pushing her will make it worse."

"She thinks you didn't want her here. She doesn't know what happened."

Suddenly it got quiet, and I was almost ready to dart back to my room, jump into bed, and pretend to be sleeping.

"How do you know that?" my dad asked.

"I do," Gail said firmly.

"From her letters? What was in those letters?"

"No, I told you I didn't read them. I just know. You're waiting for her to open up to you. Well, maybe it's you. Maybe you're the one who needs to open up. You're the grown-up. Stop being so afraid."

I heard my dad's footsteps, and I heard the TV click on. They were still talking, but I couldn't hear anymore.

My dad, afraid? My dad wasn't afraid of anything. He had answers for everything. People paid him for his answers. He had heard it all. He was tough and strong and never afraid.

Like me. I was never afraid.

But I knew I *was* afraid.

I was afraid I would never belong in this house.

I was afraid there would never be a place for me.

I was afraid of how much I missed my sister, Anne.

I crept back into bed and I wanted to fall asleep right

away. I wanted everything that had happened today to be over. I wanted it to be morning right away, so I could begin forgetting.

I didn't want to dream that night at all.

But sometimes you can't help it.

Chapter Twenty-seven

Anne had never made me feel that her mother was more hers than mine. Never. I think maybe another kid would have. I think another kid might not have been able to resist using it against me, even if it was just in a moment of anger or jealousy. Or just to get something she wanted. She had the power. She could have used it, easily.

But Anne never did. Even times when I was in trouble or times when I might not have been as nice as I could have been.

Never.

Not since the day she was born. And I remember that day, too. Long before they got divorced, a little while after they had gotten married. Maybe they had been married a year or two before they decided to have a baby (not that anyone discussed it with me or anything, but I knew a baby was coming). I was five years old, and the baby crib went up in my room one day. I remember going with my mother and her big belly to the doctor and sitting on the waiting room floor with a coloring book.

I remember it in my dreams. I can see myself coloring. I can see the book and the black and white pictures. I can see the legs of the ladies sitting all around me, with their magazines. I remember magazines.

But mostly I remember Anne. At first they put my new baby sister in their bedroom, in a little wicker basket thing on wheels, and Anne cried all the time. They moved her into her crib. She cried.

At night either my mom or dad would come in to check on her. Sometimes they carried her around or brought her back into their room. But sometimes they just let her cry, and I couldn't stand it. I figured this little baby knew I was in the room, and she was trying to get my attention. So I tried to make my body as flat as I could against my covers, so she couldn't see me. I stilled my breathing, and I didn't make a sound, not a rustle of my blankets or even a sigh. I figured if she couldn't see me, she'd have to give up.

But Anne still cried.

Then one night, I got out of my bed and I walked over to her crib. I could slip my foot into the space between the bars and hoist myself up over the top. I looked down into the crib, and Anne looked back. Her eyes were wet, and her face was all blotchy and puffy. Snot was running out of her baby nose.

She couldn't move. She couldn't wipe her nose or unwrap the blankets that were all twisted around her tiny body. She couldn't even roll over. But she was my sister.

"Shh, shh," I said. I balanced my stomach on the top bar so that I was as close as I could get. My feet were dangling in the air. I pulled the blanket out from her legs and spread it out again.

"Shh, I'm here," I said. "I was just kidding. I was here the whole time. Shh, it's okay. I'll always be here."

And she stopped crying.

Chapter Twenty-eight

Living with my mother and Anne and visiting my dad every other weekend seemed pretty ordinary to me. There were lots of divorced families. Even after Gary moved in with us, there were still *some* good times. But everything was different.

And for me, it was worse.

I don't think my dad really knew what was going on. We only visited him every other weekend. He still lived in New Paltz, and my mother and Anne and I had moved three times already.

Besides, it wasn't like my mother came home one day and said to me and Anne, "Okay girls, you know Gary? Well, he's going to be living here with us from now on. How does that sound?"

Because if it had, I would have said "That sounds awful."

Well, truthfully I wouldn't have said a thing. I didn't want her not to love me. So I never said a thing, not directly, not with words anyway. Even when things got bad.

But still, there were good times even after Gary moved in — at night when I read out loud to everyone because we didn't have a television and the nights were cold and long that winter. And that was a wonderful time.

Anne would be curled up on her mother's lap, and Gary would sit on the other end of the couch. I always sat in the rocking chair with my feet up on this giant wooden spool we used as a table.

I started with *Charlotte's Web*. I had just read the book in school, so I already knew what was going to happen. I knew how sad the ending was. So I tried to read it as well as I could. I read with feeling. If the story was funny I made it sound funny, when it was scary, I slowed down and paused and made it last as long as I could. It's all about the timing. And the emotion.

At the end of the book when Charlotte dies, they were all crying. I was choked up, too, but I had to keep reading. I did a really good job, I think, even with tears rolling down my cheeks and my voice dry and hoarse.

I was going to read all three books by E. B. White. I

took *Stuart Little* out from the library, and my dad bought me *Trumpet of the Swan* at Ariel Bookstore during one of those weekends I was visiting with him in New Paltz. I think he was just starting to date Gail then.

I couldn't wait to get back and begin reading my new book out loud to everyone.

I got better and better, and I looked forward to those nights more than I had anything else. I had one little light over my chair, and everyone else cuddled up in the shadows, listening quietly. I was the one talking. And even though it was someone else's words, I would feel what the writer was feeling, and I could feel everyone listening. To me.

It was a wonderful feeling. They were wonderful words.

Then just as quickly as spring had come and was turning to summer, it all ended. I left for sleep-away camp before I could begin *Trumpet of the Swan*. I thought I could start reading it out loud when I got back, maybe before school began in September.

But it didn't turn out that way.

I HAD MISSED ANNE so much, I had completely stopped thinking about her. I stopped talking about her, and she stopped existing. Almost. Every now and then I would be forced to remember, like when my dad would give me updates on getting visitation rights. It was hard because she was living so far away. Did he want her traveling by herself on a plane? It would have to be a direct flight.

I never wanted to hear about it.

I missed my sister so much, I tried to stop remembering her. It was all about mind control.

I was like a Hindu monk standing on one leg for years and years. And when they ask him, how do you do it? How can you stand on one leg year after year? And never put the other leg down? The Hindu monk answers, You get used to it. After a while it's like you only ever had one leg.

But two is better, he says.

Chapter Twenty-nine

"Leah, I think we should talk," my dad was saying.

I was waiting for this. I was prepared, which in retrospect, I still think is much better than improvising.

"I'm sorry about yesterday. About coming back after dark," I said. "I won't do it again. . . . And I'm sorry for what I said," I added. "I don't hate you."

I couldn't bring myself to say that I didn't hate Gail.

I was eating my cereal, talking between bites, and not having to look up. I kept pushing stubborn Cheerios back under the milk where they belonged. My bus came in ten minutes. At least this talk would have to end soon. I looked at the clock.

"Not about that." My dad was holding his coffee mug in two hands, like he didn't want it to fall, and it was about to.

"About — you," he said.

"I don't want to," I said.

"Okay," he countered. "About me, then."

I looked up.

"I made a mistake, Leah. A long time ago. I thought you'd be better off with your mother, with Karen. She was your mother, the only mother you knew. And Anne would be living with her, so it just made sense," he started talking.

"Karen called me after you left for camp and told me she was moving. To California. I think it was her boyfriend, Gary's idea, moving to California. She wanted me to take you. To live here with me and Gail. I knew she was doing a hurtful thing. To you. I knew you would be very upset," he told me.

"But at the same time, it was such a relief. A wonderful relief. It was what I had wanted all along. I never wanted to let you and Anne go. I thought I was doing what was best for you. Maybe I was wrong. I knew I had made a mistake from the start. But here was a way I could fix it. At least that's what I thought."

My ears were clogging up again. I could hear what my dad was saying, but it sounded muffled and amplified at the same time. Like in a scary movie just before something really bad happens. But nothing happened. My dad was just talking again.

"I tried to tell you about the lawyers and the hearing,"

my dad went on. "Well, it is very complicated, but Anne will be visiting us soon. I didn't want to mention anything yet, but, well, I'm trying to get Anne to live here most of the year. Go to school here. With you. And visit her mother for vacations and summer. I think that will be the best thing for her, too."

My dad wasn't looking at me. He was staring into his coffee.

"I don't ever want you to think I didn't want you," he said to his mug. "I've always wanted you. You and your sister are the most important things in my life. Even if I don't always show it."

It didn't explain anything. It didn't stop my anger or my sadness or my fear. It didn't explain why my mother had left without a word. Why she took Anne and not me. It didn't explain anything.

But there was something about the way he looked, the way he didn't know what to say. And I could tell that he loved me.

I always knew that.

Maybe that was going to have to be enough.

Chapter Thirty

I didn't get to see Will before first period. His bus always arrived at school later than mine. He rode one of those little half-buses because not that many kids lived where he did. I found out that Esopus is really far. It's halfway over the Shawangunk Mountains, which is an Indian name. Like Minnewaska and Mohonk and lots of places around here that sound like mysterious and nearly forgotten times.

I couldn't wait to talk to him, but I knew I'd have to wait until lunch. I wanted to tell him tell what happened when I got home, how I had tried to call, but my dad beat me to it. I hoped he didn't get in trouble for being late. But mostly I wanted to tell him, I was all right. That I didn't care about the audition anymore. I mean, that much anymore. I got over it.

I didn't want him to turn down a part, if he got one. I mean, I was sure he got one. I'd be so happy for him.

"Okay, everybody take your seats." It was Mrs. Thomsen. "We have a lot to do today. The marking period ends this week. Report cards will be going home Monday."

There were a couple of groans from around the room. Mine was more like a puff of air escaping from my nose, more of a resignation than a groan.

"First, I want to wrap up our unit on poetry," Mrs. Thomsen was talking away. "I hope you've enjoyed some of the poems and poets we've read."

I was thinking about the things my dad told me. He told me having strong feelings is not a bad thing. And for all the hard times and sad feelings, there are just as many wonderful feelings. It's like a double-edged sword, he said.

"And a lot of you wrote some wonderful poetry yourselves," Mrs. Thomsen went on.

My dad told me someday I'd be able to use all the feelings I was having. He said life would be harder for me, but one day I'd find it was worth it.

There can be moments of incredible joy, my dad said.

When I asked him how he could be so sure, he said he wasn't.

"I'm just going to read one of my favorites out loud," Mrs. Thomsen said and she began to read. "Left in the shadowy place that once was / Empty windows and fallen lumber / Gone are the busy sounds / Of days gone by . . ."

It took me a second — but no — yes.

It was my poem.

Mrs. Thomsen was reading my poem out loud. The heat rushed up into my face, and I tried not to move, not to give it away. I tried not to smile, but I couldn't help it.

Mrs. Thomsen read the whole thing.

"That was a really good poem, Mrs. Thomsen," a girl in the front of the room said. I think her name was Caroline. Caroline was a goody-two-shoes.

"Yeah," another kid said.

"What's it about?"

"Whose was it?"

"It's Leah's," Mrs. Thomsen said, and she smiled right at me. Everyone turned around at the same time and looked.

I looked at Mrs. Thomsen for a quick minute and smiled back. Then I lowered my head and shrugged.

"Now, we are going to move on to short stories. And I have vocabulary books to pass out," Mrs. Thomsen said.

A couple more groans.

"I'll help," Caroline said, raising her hand.

"Thank you," Mrs. Thomsen said.

Caroline got up, and Mrs. Thomsen moved back to her desk. The moment had passed, my moment. And then again, it hadn't. It was stuck in my head and in my heart.

I think I was having one of those "moments of incredible joy."

Chapter Thirty-one

And when the class was over, Sasha Buckley was waiting for me in the hall.

"Your poem sucked," she said.

"Glad you liked it," I said, and I barely had time to be proud of what a good response that was.

"Are you deaf? I said, it sucked."

At this point, I decided walking past was my best move. Sasha was bigger than I was.

"You know, you're really weird," Sasha said to my back. "You're going to meet your boyfriend again, aren't you?"

I kept walking.

"In the auditorium, aren't you?" she called after me.

I was still walking.

"Will Hiller's a faggot, you know," Sasha said.

I stopped and turned to face her. Sasha was standing there, with one hand on her hip. Her eyes were narrow and shifting from side to side. She had a very familiar pinched expression on her face.

There was a little girl who had a little curl
Right in the middle of her forehead.

I could almost see a little curl slipping from Sasha's ponytail. I opened my mouth to say something, something good, but there was nothing to say.

"You look like a fish with your mouth open like that," Sasha said.

I shut my mouth, and I walked away.

⋘⋙

"WILL, DO YOU KNOW who Sasha Buckley is?" I asked.

"Yeah, she rides my bus," Will said.

We were both sitting on the edge of the stage, swinging our legs out and letting our heels hit the hollow-sounding wood.

"She does?"

"Yeah, she lives on my road," Will started. "We were in kindergarten together. She used to play at my house. She's really good at kickball. She used to be pretty nice."

"What happened?"

Will laughed. "She doesn't like you, huh?"

"She hates me. And she's going to tell on us," I began. "She saw us come in here. She knows we come in here at recess."

"She won't tell," Will said. He stopped banging his feet against the stage. "Sasha may be a lot of things, but she'd never tell."

"How do you know?"

"Trust me. I just know. She rides my bus. And she doesn't hate you," Will said. "She hates herself."

I thought about that. And then I thought about my poem, and how good I felt when Mrs. Thomsen read it out loud. How lucky I was to have that. And how I would try really hard to never let that feeling fade away.

I was going to tell Will about it, but I stopped myself. He was so excited about the play. The cast list was going to be put up this afternoon before last period. I was thinking about Will and how important this was for him. How much I wished it for him. I really did.

"You're going to get a part, you know," I told Will. "And when Mr. Calabrini sees how good you are, you'll get a bigger part."

Will started banging his feet again, but softly. "Maybe we'll both get a part."

"Maybe," I said. "But if you get a part and I don't, you have to be in the play."

"I know," Will said.

We sat still for a while. The bell would ring any minute.

"You know, Leah," Will started, "you're different than anybody I've ever been friends with."

It was the greatest of compliments.

"So are you," I said quietly.

Chapter Thirty-two

I didn't look for my name on the cast list. School was dismissed, and I walked right by it, out the door to the bus loop. I could just make out the top of three white sheets stuck on the wall by the office. There were too many people around there anyway, heads peering over one another, a little pushing, a couple of squeals of excitement. I hurried past.

But I rode the bus all the way home wondering if I should have looked.

Maybe if I had seen Will there, we could have looked together. But it could wait. Or Will would call me.

I could certainly wait to find out what I already knew.

Nobody was home when I got off the bus, and I was relieved. I was thankful I hadn't decided to tell my dad or

Gail about the audition. I didn't have to tell anyone any-thing. I didn't have to mention that I didn't get a part in the middle-school play.

And then when I felt like it, maybe I could tell them about my poem.

Maybe even add a little bit to my story, like how Mrs. Thomsen cried when she read it, or how everyone came up to me after class and asked me about it. Where did I get the idea? How long did it take to write?

Not lying. Just a little creative license.

All of a sudden I couldn't wait to tell someone. I could hardly stand it. I wanted so badly to tell my dad that I might even tell Gail if she was home. No sense in keep-ing it a secret, stashed away in a drawer, like a piece of folded lace. Pink and white.

❧

MY ROOM IN SHANDAKEN wasn't really a room, it was like the top of an attic where the ceiling slanted down. There was only enough space for my bed and a small bu-reau. When we moved there, Anne got the big room and we put all our toys in there. It made sense. She was younger and played with them a lot. She still liked to make tents and play dress-up. So I got to have the little room, the little but more grown-up room.

To get to my room you had to go through Anne's

room and through a little door, a really little door. It made my room seem almost magical. Like the room where a fairy or a hidden princess might live.

Only I lived there. It was my room.

So most of stuff, my CDs and CD player, all of my books (all of them), my stuffed animals, and all my toys, and all the things I had saved, I kept in Anne's room. In her room there were two built-in shelves against the wall. One was for me, and one was for Anne. We played in Anne's room most of the time, anyway. We spread out all our Little People on the floor. We built Little People worlds and had Little People adventures.

It was while I was at camp, my dad came to take all my things, when my mother called him and told him to take me — I suppose he didn't know. I suppose my mother made sure she wasn't home when he came to get my things. He didn't know about everything I had on the shelf in Anne's room — and so he left all my stuff there.

I guess he just didn't know.

I WALKED RIGHT OVER to my bureau. When things get hidden away, they aren't protected, they're lost.

I opened the top drawer and reached inside.

I had to feel around in the back. It had been a while, and lots of socks and underwear had come and gone from this drawer. I felt what I was looking for, hidden away in the back, crumpled up and smushed in the corner, almost lost.

I pulled out the long piece of lace my mother had given me.

I shook it out, and I lay it down carefully on my bed. Then slowly, I began to take everything off my bureau. I took off my CD player and CDs and the blue jewelry box with all the mirrors. I took the pictures Will had made for me and lay them on my bed, too. Everything I had collected. All my stuff.

When the top of the bureau was empty, I wiped the dust with my sleeve of my shirt and then I carefully spread the lace on top. It had rows of pink and white stitching, so I could make sure it hung equally from each end, just the way it had been before.

It was pretty, and it looked good in my room. I knew the light from the sun might fade the colors over time, and if I put everything back on top, the delicate lace might even get pulled or torn. And I knew one day, I might not even want this piece of lace on top of my bureau anymore. But for now, I ran my hand across and smoothed it out, and I put everything back on top. All my stuff. I gave it one final adjustment, and then I stood back. It looked all right.

This was my room now. I was nearly sure.

I was home.

Chapter Thirty-three

I knew it was Will's mother almost immediately, even though Mrs. Hiller had much lighter coloring than Will. And even though Will's mother was short and kind of heavy and looked nothing like him. They smiled exactly the same smile. They stood with the same lean to one side, crossed arms. But mostly it was the way they stood together.

The way the space between them was only space, not distance. You could just feel it, how comfortable they were together. How they belonged together.

It made me think of the lichen.

Although, at first I was mixed-up by the whole thing. What were Will and his mother doing in my house?

They all walked in at the same time, Will and Mrs. Hiller and Gail, about twenty minutes after I had gotten home. I was watching TV in the living room, but I got up when everybody starting coming in.

"Oh, Leah," Gail said.

She was carrying grocery bags in both arms, followed by Will, who was also carrying a bag, and then the short woman, so obviously Will's mother, who was also carrying a grocery bag.

"I'm sorry I'm late. I was shopping," Gail said, and then she laughed. "And look who was coming down the driveway right after me?"

Gail put the bags down on the counter, and Will did the same. "We introduced ourselves in the driveway. But I thought I recognized Will's voice from the phone," Gail was saying.

Will was smiling. Mrs. Hiller held out her hand to me.

"I'm Will's mother," she said. "You must be Leah."

She was beautiful, just like Will.

"Hi," I said.

Will was still smiling, stupid smiling. Huge smiling.

"What?" I said. "What's going on?"

"We came to get you," Will said. "To celebrate."

"Celebrate what?"

What was going on?

"Leah, you got a part," Will said. He started jumping, but his feet stayed on the ground. He was sort of jumping and sort of trying not to jump.

"A part in a play?" Gail asked. "Were there auditions?"

Mrs. Hiller nodded. "Yes, and Will didn't even mention anything about it, until today. Until he saw the cast list. Then he asked me if we could take Leah out to celebrate. If that's okay?"

"Oh, Leah that's terrific. I thought something was up," Gail said. "But I thought something was wrong. I thought you were upset about something."

"I was," I said. "I mean, I can't believe it. Are you sure? Maybe it is someone else."

"Positive," Will said. "It was your name. Leah Baer. B-A-E-R. I remember, because I didn't know that's how you spelled your name. Well, it's not a big part or anything. But so what, right?"

"Yeah, so what?" I said.

"You don't have a name, like a character or anything. Neither do I," Will went on.

"But it's worth celebrating," Mrs. Hiller said.

"Absolutely," Gail said.

"So do you want to go?" Will asked.

I looked toward Gail. I had never asked her permission for anything before. I still didn't want to, but I did. I thought I should.

"Can I?" I asked.

"Of course, go," Gail said. She almost looked happier than I did.

I turned back to Will. "Really?"

"Yes, c'mon already," Will said.

"Okay," I said. I ran to get my jacket from my room. I took one last look around my room. My jacket was right on the floor where I had left it. My stuff was all around my room. My room was all around me. And I knew I was in the right place. I ran back out to the kitchen. They were waiting for me.

"Uh, Mrs. Hiller?" I started. "Do you think maybe . . . I mean, Gail don't you want to come, too?"

Gail stopped what she was doing. She turned around.

"Oh, Leah. It's okay, really," she said. "Mrs. Hiller *did* ask me if I wanted to go, but you guys go out. Really, I'm okay. I've got a lot to do here." She waved her hand around the kitchen.

I looked down at my shoes.

"But I do appreciate your asking. Really." Gail added. "It means a lot to me."

"Well, whatever you two decide," Mrs. Hiller said quickly. "We'll meet you outside." She opened the outside door and held it. "I'm going to go warm up the car. C'mon, Will."

"You left the car running, Mom," Will said. He crinkled his brow, then uncrinkled it. "Yeah, we'll be outside." And Will followed his mother out through the kitchen door.

Gail sat down in one of the chairs by the little table.

"Really, Leah. I'm okay. I mean, I'm not going to break any more dishes." She smiled and kind of laughed.

"No, it's not like that," I said. "I just thought . . . if you want to come, I'd really like it."

And suddenly, I really wanted her to come. I mean, I think I did.

"You do?" Gail asked.

I nodded. I did.

It was that easy.

Dear Mom,

I know I haven't written to you in a long time but this time it was on purpose. Because I have something to say.

But first, I'll just let you know I am very busy with play rehearsals. I don't have a very big part. In fact, I barely have a part at all. In fact, I'm a boy in the play. Apparently, there aren't a lot of boys who try out and some girls have to be boys. I think everyone who tried out got a part. But it doesn't matter. I'm having a good time.

Will is in the play. He started out with a small part too but now he has more. I have two lines. I say "run" and "I don't know." Will took over the part of some 7th grader who got Mono. (that's mononucleosis) The first performance is December 15th.

Oh, hey get this — remember that girl, Sasha, who used to hate me? Well she's in the play too.

156

She isn't <u>in</u> the play but she works up on the catwalk because her older brother runs the lights. I tried the paradox on her. And it worked! I started being really nice to her. I wouldn't say we are friends or anything. But at least she doesn't hate me. As much. Anymore.

Things can really change, even things you never thought would.

In fact, I've changed so much that I don't think you'd recognize me. I've grown three inches and I weigh 80 pounds now. Like I told you, my hair got really long and then, you'd never believe, last week Gail took me to a beauty shop and I got it all cut off. All of it. I felt like a hundred pounds came right off my head. I feel like I can fly. I love it. When I look in the mirror I don't think I'm so out of proportion. My head looks about right. And my body seems to fit.

Dad says I look like Audrey Hepburn and when I said I didn't know who that was, he said "How 'bout Rachel Leigh Cook?"

"In what movie?" I asked him.

"<u>Josie and the Pussycats</u>."

That was a good movie.

Still, sometimes I lay in my bed at night and I make myself this kind of dream. I dream that I will bump into you on the street one day, in New York or California. I will be really famous and everything will be wonderful for me. Or I will be a writer or an actress or a singer so you will know who I am because you've seen my name or read one of my books. And you'll recognize me from my picture in the back of the book. And when you finally read one of my poems or my novel you'll know how I felt. You'll understand.

And I'll stop when I see you, because you seem familiar. And I'll look right into your eyes. I'll see something I remember from a long time ago but it won't hurt anymore. I won't even remember what it felt like so long ago.

I'll just smile with that look of vague recognition and walk away. And you'll feel bad for everything you did.

I give myself that dream even though I know it's not nice, and anger just weighs you down like a whole head of hair, like a a pound of rocks strapped to your back. It gives you a pinched, horrid face.

So I don't have that dream anymore.

Then other times, I give myself a totally different dream, where you come back and tell me how sorry you are. How it was a big mistake and you never meant to hurt me. You want to see me again, I'll be your daughter and everything will be okay. You hold out your arms and we hug for a really long time to make up for all the time we were apart.

But that dream hurts more than anything, much more.

Now, I try to dream about totally different things all together. Like school — I'm getting a B in language arts and a B in social studies. Mrs. Thomsen says I could get an A if I wanted. I'm getting a D in math but oh, well. I dream about the play, and about Will, and me.

Right now, I am just waiting for Anne to come. Dad and I are picking her up at the airport tomorrow. Maybe that's why I am writing again after so long.

I wanted to say good bye.

Good bye.

love, Leah

Chapter Thirty-four

My dad and I drove to the airport by ourselves. Gail stayed home to cook something special. She asked me what Anne liked to eat. I couldn't think of anything. All I could remember was that Anne never complained. She ate whatever she was given.

Unlike me.

"Oh, Anne likes anything," I told Gail.

Then as we were walking out the door I had a second thought. "Except zucchini," I said. "She hates zucchini."

It was about a two-hour drive to the airport in New York City.

"I'm a little nervous," my dad said. "How about you?"

This was another one of my dad's psychology ploys. I don't know if it had ever worked on me, maybe to get me to tell him why I was crying or something when I was really little.

The trick was that he would pretend to be sharing some feeling he was having, when in reality it was some feeling he assumed *I* was having. I was supposed to fall for that and think — Wow, what a coincidence! I feel the exact same way. This was supposed to make me burst out talking about *my* feelings, so he could help me sort it all out.

"Really?" I said. "You need to talk about it?"

He laughed.

"Fair enough," he said. "But I *am* a little nervous. It's been a long time since we've seen Anne. Remember when you guys used to come visit me. Before Gail. When I lived in that little apartment?"

Of course I remembered. My dad made the best jelly omelettes. But that was all he made. And then he moved on to fish sticks and chicken pot pies. He got to be a pretty good cook, before he married Gail. Gail is definitely a better cook.

"Yeah, we slept on those cots," I said.

I could see the gray landscape, billboards, and tall buildings. Soon I could see the belly of airplanes flying low over the highway. We would be at the airport in a few minutes.

"It was always so hard for me when you left," my dad

was saying. "When the weekend was over and you went back."

It was the worst.

The funny thing was, I never wanted to go to his apartment on Friday in the first place. I used to complain that the drive was too long, and there was nothing to do. I think, some of it was for the benefit of Anne's mother/Karen/Mom. I wanted to sound like I didn't care. I wanted her to know I preferred her over my dad. I was afraid.

But by Sunday night, after the weekend at my dad's, I didn't want to go back.

I couldn't win. Going or not going.

"It was hard for me, too, Dad," I said. I kept looking out the window. We had just gotten off the ramp for La-Guardia Airport.

"It was?"

"Yeah," I said.

We took the exit for arriving flights/short-term parking.

"I'm glad," my dad said.

❧

THE ELECTRONIC BOARD inside the building said that Anne's flight was on time. Only, none of this seemed to be on time. It was late. It was long overdue. In fact, it was all wrong.

I shouldn't have been sitting in an airport waiting for

my sister. She shouldn't have been on a plane all by herself. I thought, *Anne must be so scared*. She is so small and
quiet. She's seven, but knowing Anne she wouldn't even
tell anyone if she had to use the bathroom or if she was
thirsty. She's too young for all this. She should be with
me, so I could watch out for her. Like I used to.

A whole lot of people got off the plane. There was a
lot of hugging and kissing. Lots of big people and little
people and strollers and suitcases. When it had pretty
much cleared, the flight attendant walked off with Anne
right next to her. There she was. Anne had this huge tag
hanging around her neck. She didn't see us right away.

She *was* small. And she *did* look scared. She had her
shirt tucked into her elastic waist pants, and it was all
bunched up around her middle. It made her look like she
had a big, huge belly. She had a floppy, little hat on her
head. She was holding a straw bag in her hand. She
looked hilarious.

I broke out laughing.

She turned her head quickly, and she saw me. I saw her
tug the sleeve of the woman in the uniform and point
toward us. They both walked over.

"What?" Anne said. She looked down at her pants.
"What?"

"Your pants," I said to Anne. "Look."

Anne looked down and laughed. "Oh, ha! Look, I'm
fat," she said. She patted her belly.

Then without another word, she stepped over to Dad and lay her head against his body. He wrapped his arms around her, and they stayed like that.

The flight attendant smiled. "I suppose you are . . ."

"Jeff," my dad said, still hugging Anne. "Jeff Baer."

Anne looked out at me from under Dad's big arms. She smiled. She had tears in her eyes.

"I'm sorry," she said so quietly.

"It wasn't your fault," I whispered back.

The flight attendant said that our dad just had to show some ID, and then sign something. He let go, stopped hugging to reach for his wallet. Anne took the two or three steps to be next to me.

"I'm just glad you're here," I told my sister.

"Me, too, but I'm scared," Anne said. "And I miss Mom."

We stood next to each other while all the grown-ups sorted things out.

"I know, but everything is going to be all right," I told my sister. "Trust me."

"I do," Anne said.

Chapter Thirty-five

*E*ven when particular things (and most people around us), were confusing and sometimes scary, my sister and I always had our Little People. When we picked Anne up at the airport and then drove back, it was the first thing she showed me. She had a little bag in her suitcase and inside were our Little People.

"I couldn't bring everyone," Anne told me. "And I couldn't bring any blocks or houses or cars. I couldn't bring the school bus."

There was a moment of pain again, thinking about our toys, toys I had played with, built with, put away when I was done. Those blocks and cars and the houses being so far away. How they were in Anne's new room, that I would never see. I pushed the feeling away. I had to, at least for now. The wall between wanting to understand, what or why my mother had done what she did, and needing to move on was still so high.

It might even be as high as infinity.

My dad tells me there isn't an explanation for everything. That doesn't mean you have to stop thinking about things, but you might have to accept them. Accept that there are some things you'll just never get a good answer for. Hmmm.

Anne dumped the bag out on the ground in my room. Dad had set up her old cot right next to my bed, but there was still plenty of room on the rug. Everyone came spilling out as well as a hundred memories. When Anne and I played Little People the whole world would disappear. We would shrink and shrink smaller and smaller, until all I remember of our playing were the families and their houses and their cars, but not our big hands moving them around in the street.

Everyone had a family, and even if every time we switched people or got different toys, their families had to stay together. We would take turns choosing people and, of course, there were the favorites. Cowboy Boy was a favorite, probably because he was cute, and he wasn't missing any facial features. But sometimes it was the more worn and dejected characters we favored. Red-haired girl with the red freckles, whose one pigtail had been chewed off was always one of the first picked. So was the too-long-in-the-bathtub mom who had lost most of her painted-on face.

Some of the figures were not plastic, but little animals or little fast-food-giveaways that we especially liked. It was almost like they had their own personalities, we had played with them so much and for so long. When Anne poured them out again, it almost came back to me.

At first, when Anne got here I *wanted* to play. We set up a little town just like we used to. We used shoe boxes and pillows and baskets from the kitchen. We made a town, with homes and a school and a hospital. No town was complete without a hospital, since our playing most always involved a natural disaster or two. We divided up all the figures Anne had brought, and then something happened.

I *didn't* want to play. I couldn't.

"What's wrong?" Anne asked me. She had her little guy poised above the school ready for the day to begin.

"I don't know," I said. "I don't feel like playing any-more."

"But we just started."

"I know," I said.

I sat back on my knees, away from our Little People town. I knew right away, it was no use. In order to play, in order to *really* play — you have to believe. You have to be able to give up this world for that one. You have to

give up the real world, at least for the time you are playing. And before I had even begun, I knew I couldn't.

I was too big. I was too old. If I tried to play, I would
be faking it, like watching myself pretending instead of
really pretending.

"So you don't want to play?" Anne asked me.

I felt bad, but I shook my head.

"But I'll stay in the room," I said. "And when you're
done I'll have an earthquake with you."

"How about a tornado?"

"Sure, a tornado," I agreed. "And then I'll help you
clean up."

"Okay," Anne said.

I jumped up onto my bed, and I read the book I had
been reading, and I listened to Anne's little voice below
me. It didn't distract me at all. It felt just right. And
when she was ready, we had a really good storm. The
Little People families all ran for cover, searched high and
low, and didn't give up until they had found each other.
They fell into each other's arms (even though Fisher-
Price figures don't have any arms) and cried. There were
casualties and heroes. They all vowed to build a new and
better life, even amid all the rubble that had been their
town.

I thought about asking Anne what happened to all my
stuff. What happened to my CDs and my stuffed animals. I wanted to ask her about my books, about *Trumpet*

of the Swan and *Charlotte's Web* and all the others. But I didn't. I didn't want to upset or put her in the middle or make her feel bad.

Anyway, it didn't matter. It was all gone and all of it was only stuff anyway. I looked around my room. You can always get more stuff.

Chapter Thirty-six

> **NEW PALTZ MIDDLE SCHOOL**
> **is proud to present**
> *Welcome to the Monkey House*
> **by Kurt Vonnegut Jr.**
> **adapted and directed by Don Calabrini**

I wasn't as nervous as I thought I'd be. I didn't have that much to do after all. I was so amazed by the other actors. Especially Will. When Will got on stage he was like another person. He totally transformed. His voice, his face. The way he stood and walked. He was most definitely a talent. He was different from everybody else.

Will was so definitely going to be something when he grew up. Famous, even. But certainly something special, I knew it.

"I'm nervous," Will said to me.

We were both in the boys' bathroom in the hall by the music rooms. During the play we were allowed to use either bathroom for putting on makeup. The bathrooms behind the dressing rooms were for going to the bathroom, if you had to really go to the bathroom. It seemed that right before the show was to go on, a lot of people had to use the bathroom for that purpose. Mr. Calabrini said it was excitement.

"You're not nervous," he told the cast just an hour ago. "You're excited. Think of it that way and you'll be fine."

"You're excited," I told Will. We were both staring at ourselves in the wide mirror above the three sinks.

"No, I'm definitely nervous," Will said.

He was putting another layer of powder over his pancake makeup. He had eyeliner under his dark eyes and even red color brushed onto his cheekbones. The makeup mothers assured us that onstage you would barely see it.

I could see my reflection beside Will's. A little less pinched, a little less angry. Me, Leah Baer, getting ready to go onstage with all the lights glaring from above, muffled noises from the hundred or so people in the velvet seats. Ushers were walking up and down the aisles. The program had my name in it, even if it was way down at the bottom.

"So, okay. You're nervous. But you're going to be great," I said.

I watched my lip-sticked mouth moving in the mirror.

"I might mess up," Will said.

"You might. But I doubt it," I said.

Will was pushing his hair back with his fingers. He stopped.

"You know," he began. "It couldn't get any better than this."

I did know.

And it was really funny, because I was almost thinking the exact same thing. I mean, what could be better? We had everything in front of us. The opening of this show felt like the opening of my life. The set might fall down, and someone might drop a line or two (dropping a line is theater talk for forgetting what you're supposed to say). It might be me, in fact. In fact, it probably was going to be me.

Being in the show did make you nervous, and it made you excited. And Will and I were in it together. Will's mom and dad and his sister were in the audience. My dad was here, of course, and Anne, who had stayed the extra week so she could see the show. It seemed that maybe she *was* going to be living with us. She was going to be flying back to California this weekend. I didn't want to think about that. Not now.

It was harder for Anne. She had terrible stomachaches while she was here. She even went to the hospital in Kingston once, and the doctor said it was nothing. Warm liquids, dry toast, and a heating pad, he told us.

It was not *nothing*. It was everything, but I know she's going to be okay.

She's got me.

"I mean, this very second," Will said. "I can't imagine it could get any better than this."

Will looked from the mirror, from his reflection. He turned to me.

It would have been silly for me to keep staring into the mirror, looking at Will looking at me. I took my eyes from the mirror and looked at Will, and we were stuck like that for that very long moment. Then Will took a deep breath.

"You know what I mean?" he said softly.

I nodded.

I knew what Will meant. We had our whole lives ahead of us, but what we shared in that space, in that time, in that exact moment, was so wonderful.

I was sure.

Reader's Guide

1. What are some of the different kinds of "family" in *Almost Home* and how does Leah's understanding of what makes a family change?

2. How is Leah's behavior and performance in school related to her emotional struggles at home? Does the relationship change throughout the novel?

3. How important are play and imagination to Leah? How do these needs manifest themselves and change throughout the course of the book?

4. Why does Leah write letters to her "mother"? Do you think she ever intended to mail them?

5. What role does Will Hiller play in Leah's life? What are some of the things he teaches her and how?

6. How is the piece of lace given to Leah by her mother symbolic? Does that symbolism remain the same or change by the end of the book?

7. What is the significance of Leah's "stuff"? What does it mean to her and how does its importance change?

8. Why is Leah reluctant to commit herself to the school play? How is that reluctance connected to her mother?

9. Acceptance is a major theme of this book. Do you think acceptance comes from a position of strength or of giving up?

10. Look for all the situations in which Leah's poem appears in her life. How is it a symbol of her growth?

11. Some of Leah's fondest memories with her sister, Anne, are of playing and creating new worlds. What does it mean when Anne comes to visit and Leah realizes she can't play anymore?

12. Leah admits that she never let her mother know her true feelings about Gary or about their constant moving. Why is she so quick to let Gail know how she feels about her when she never did the same with her mother?

Nora Raleigh Baskin is the author of the acclaimed *What Every Girl (except me) Knows.* She grew up in Brooklyn and New Paltz, New York, and now lives in Connecticut with her husband and two boys. *Almost Home* is her second novel.

PRAISE FOR
What Every Girl (except me) Knows:

★ "A bittersweet, emotionally complex novel. Baskin sensitively renders the tumultuous period between childhood and adolescence."
—*Publishers Weekly,* starred review

R "Perceptive and sympathetic. Gabby and Taylor's friendship is absolutely authentic."
—*Bulletin for the Center for Children's Books,* recommended book

"A gripping coming-of-age story and the painful family mystery are a winning combination."
—*Booklist*

"Candid, lively, and absorbing. A fine novel that offers a perspective and positive look at dealing with loss."
—*School Library Journal*